For Kosi
with all my
affection

THE SPOIL OF THE FLOWERS

The Spoil
of the Flowers

DORIS GRUMBACH

DOUBLEDAY & COMPANY, INC.

Garden City, New York, 1962

For the four sisters who are my daughters,
    their father,
        and the Sisters of St. Joseph of
        Carondelet who are my friends

Εἰς τὸν λειμῶνα καθίσας,
ἔδρεπεν ἕτερον ἐφ᾽ ἑτέρῳ
αἰρόμενος ἄγρευμ᾽ ἀνθέων
ἡδομένᾳ ψυχᾷ.

> He sat in the meadow and plucked with
> glad heart the spoil of the flowers,
> gathering them one by one.
> —EURIPIDES. *Fragment*

Because this novel is a parable some persons will see themselves in these characters and be angry at what they find. Others will be sure they recognize the institution. If this happens, however, the parable succeeds in its first purpose of being immediately applicable, in some respect or other, to each reader. But at the same time it will be a false identification. These people are not based on live models, and no single institution is portrayed.

CHAPTER I

Faculty House

For May 24, 196—, items from Ellen Acton's notebook, written on the narrow-ruled back pages of her spiral roll book:

Today the final senior English class for the year. *Gott sei dank!* The girls were wild, almost hysterical. Nan Kittredge revealed a football letter "A" colored red pinned to her blouse during my review questions on the last chapter of *The Scarlet Letter.* Occasion for enormous hilarity. Two other sports recited sixty Pope couplets from *Essay of Man* to the accompaniment of bongo drums. Rather an improvement over my reading, I thought, but did not tell them so.

Poor Sophie. I must do something for her (about her?). But every time I gird my moral loins I find I can't approach her. I'm afraid I'll unstop the whole frightening, pent-up plumbing, and I'm just as afraid I won't be able to cope with what comes forth.

Why do I stand frozen and craven before any display of human emotion? Do I distrust it as melodramatic—or false? Or is it that I am inadequate to anything but the surface spoutings of polite, everyday intercourse?

Edmund Wilson says that "art has its origin in the need to pretend that human life is something other than it is." This must be why I flee to literature. I cannot face the rawness of the real world, and so I resort to the warmed-over flavor of literature.

Do all English teachers think they are writers, pretend they will be, keep journals, dislike teaching as an economic stopgap? One night last week I woke up with an opening sentence for a short story: *He lived alone in an old house with a wife who had died and two children who had left him.* For a moment it seemed inspired. Then I could think of no place to go with it. In the morning all I remembered, beside the sentence, was that years ago Tess Schlesinger wrote a story with that line in it. I read too much, talk too much—there's nothing left in me to write, if ever indeed there was anything.

Last night was a fiasco. Can Sophie recover? Can I? If the students knew any of *Merchant* by heart they gave no evidence of it. Shakespeare was last night's medium of attack; they chose their weapons well. Sophie prodded the Seniors out on the stage, hopefully, naively, to make iambic pentameter fools of themselves, and they seemed to lean into the wings to belittle her teaching, satirize her coaching. Like Duncan's horses, "'tis said they eat each other." I tried to scowl them into behaving, and only wished I had the courage to lower the curtain and keep it down after four minutes of the first act.

I believe Sappho was the first headmistress: address all inquiries to The Headmistress, Aeolian School for Girls, Lesbos (advertisment in the educational pages of *The New York Times*).

I think I'll try to get to Mass tomorrow. Mass of the Roman Saint Gregory, according to my missal which quotes him as saying: "I have loved justice and hated iniquity. That is why I die

in exile." A thought for tomorrow's Disciplinary meeting. Maybe
I'll fortify my spirit with early Mass before it.

Duc de la Rochefoucauld: "We promise according to our
hopes; we perform according to our fears."

Faculty House on the campus of Miss Hands School for
Girls stands almost in the shadow of the new Arts Hall. A
thin, clapboard Victorian afterthought to the American Gothic
of the earlier buildings, and a neglected ancestor of the shaved-
looking hollow triangle that was Arts Hall, it housed the resi-
dent faculty in a series of rooms whose flattened rectangular
shapes were the result of cutting down each original, spacious
bedroom into three small ones. This process of division pro-
duced rooms which Ellen Acton, English Mistress, thought of
as symbolic of the atmosphere of the school: squeezed, narrow, restricted, airless. And Robbie Parks would say in her flat
Radcliffe voice every night as the Headmistress flicked the
sitting-room lights in warning: "Sisters, let us adjourn to our
cells."
Early on the Saturday morning of the suicide Miss Acton
sat alone in the downstairs sitting room. The heat was already
heavy, and she had, before she settled herself with her coffee
cup, pulled back the heavy drapes to let in the morning air.
The end of May lay like a blanket upon the campus; it seemed
compounded of the entire semester of heated games, overwrought, confessional themes, and the tensions of senior admissions into college. Arriving in mid-month, these acceptances
and rejections combined with the rising warmth of young grass
and freshly lined tennis courts, bared arms and anxieties about
the arrival of parents for Commencement Week to create an
unbearably oppressive atmosphere. The school seemed at this
moment too small for the strength of adolescent emotions and
hostile to the pressures of a summer prematurely upon it.
Ellen stirred her metallic coffee and considered the morning.

Because she could not bring herself to take the first drink, she stirred again, sipped a little, shuddered. The morning had a patina of freedom, but under scrutiny turned out to be almost as determinedly scheduled as the five days behind her. *But still, thank God, it is Saturday, crowded yes, but not totally organized.* The coffee restored her; she felt grateful for the respite.

Stirring fitfully at the dregs Ellen made a mental list. *Last chapel, unusual for Saturday, some sort of horrible rehearsal. Last meeting for the year of the Disciplinary Committee: oh Holy Saint Jude (a fitting invocation), Trudy Langer again. . . . See about the ten dollars Sophie owes me. . . . Check the book closet for fugitive copies of* Macbeth. . . . It always amazed Ellen to observe how reluctant the juniors were to return their copies despite their stubborn resistance to its poetry during the three endless weeks they studied it.

Morning coffee was not ready in the Buttery until eight-thirty. There the faculty had to sit dispersed at the Girls Tables, each one to eight half-dressed, sullen, half-asleep pupils. Ellen found it easier to face them if she armed herself first with a half-hour of privacy, silence and coffee. Unsavory as it was, she gazed into the remains of water dotted with sulphur—powdered coffee, synthetic consolation, with bits of metallic salts dissolved from the plug-in coil she had used to heat the water.

Her usual early-morning chair was behind the oak door. From it she was cut off from the sitting room, and from the hall and front door as well. Opposite her the wall was lined with former headmistresses of Miss Hands, and Miss Hands herself, painted by an ambitious but untalented mother of one of her first pupils, as a gift of the Class of 1829. Miss Hands sat permanentized, stiffly posed, an open Bible placed righteously on her lap, her eyes fixed on some small invisible sinner before her. Ellen always found Miss Hands's fingers a source of amusement. Only the forefinger of the right hand seemed to have interested the painter. It was out of joint, of extraordinary length and pointed suggestively downward, while the other fingers formed a premature fist. Her left hand was obscured by the Bible; her long nose and closely set eyes reminded the assembled faculty whose weekly meetings were held beneath the portrait, of that gallant lady's nineteenth-century struggle against male domination. Miss Hands's first school, the motto beneath her portrait reminded the modern witness, was properly classic in intent. The Academe it was called at its establishment in 1825, and documents still framed on the wall reported that seven young women "of good breeding and sound intelligence" had constituted its first class. Their names followed. Beneath this optimistic estimate there appeared the slogan *Quand Même.* In the years that followed, these gallant words were to be embroidered into the pockets of white blazers, engraved on heavy bond stationery, and, despite suggestions that it be changed or modernized, chiseled into the cornerstone of the new Arts Hall.

Upstairs now she could hear the first stirrings of the faculty. Firm, quick steps: *Jo Long,* she thought. *First into the bath while it's still clean.* A great rush of water. *She is washing her hair.* Every morning, every night, Jo expiated some nameless guilt by washing her hair: it seemed to Ellen she had rarely seen it entirely dry. *Scrubbed almost to a subcutaneous layer of her being, Jo Long is upstairs, for the ten millionth time submerging her black inner self in water.*

At the other end of the long room the dark-beamed ceiling groaned twice: *the Headmistress, dressed but unwashed, looking perhaps for a shoe, discovering a small part of her hem unsewn, debating, sitting down on her bed to pin it.*

Ellen leaned back against the high carved back of her chair and closed her eyes. The cup moved uneasily in its saucer. Across the campus the carillon struck eight and went at once into its relentless pursuit of *Jam Lucis Orto Sidere.* When she opened her eyes Miss Hands's unanatomical finger was illuminated by a stroke of the sun. *She suggests I get going. Onwards and upwards to the uplifting platitudes of breakfast and Chapel.* Ellen felt herself settling into resignation, reset her face into its customary even Irish lines, and left the sitting room. Only as she closed the front door behind her and started down the path to the Buttery did she remember her resolution to go to early Mass.

The sound of the downstairs door slamming stirred the Headmistress from her lethargy. She had been sitting on her bed searching blindly under it for her other shoe. Arvilla Blount was overly tall, and reduced her height, she felt, by her habit of bending forward at the waist as if she were permanently compelled to illustrate an inhuman, one-hundred-and-sixty-degree angle. Her face, like her posture which suggested a former erectness that only time had gradually reduced to a broken line, showed traces of a once-regular beauty. Now, like a landscape over which a meandering stream has cut deeply, leaving permanent marks in the paths of its retreat, her cheeks were cut into lines flowing downward to the delta of her very pointed chin. They resumed in her neck, marring and straining the orginial white into ridges of tough, red veins. Nothing of youth was left to Miss Blount, and only her strong prejudices, formed mainly as a result of the economic exigencies of running a small, private, girls' school, with little endowment and no claim upon state or national aid, had withstood the tests of time.

Her early history had suggested a rather different path for her personality. The second of three daughters of an earnest and everlastingly frightened minister in Northern Vermont, whose professed Congregational faith was heavily coated with a stern Puritanism of earlier vintage, she was by nature (and from her mother's example, perhaps) mild, gentle, retiring and easily frightened. Her father's decisions and opinions she made her own, mistaking them always for evidences of her own free will. Her easy acquiescence grew out of an eagerness to be loved out of all proportion to her middle position in the family of girls. In high school she was hardly noticed, although the English teacher, aware of her persistent desire to do well everything assigned to her, and of her vast ignorance of English grammar, responded to the gentle girl's unspoken need and, in unusually strong terms, recommended her to Bryn Mawr College.

Only when they realized that she, of all their girls, was the one who was certain to leave home, did her father and mother discover their affection for her, and reveal it. Her mother's took homey forms: "Arvilla, are you certain the three camisoles are enough?" Her father studied the college's catalogue with great care, and selected her courses. He then turned to the calendar at the front and noted the date of the first scheduled vacation. He laid plans well in advance for his curate to take over for him when he went down to Pennsylvania to call for his daughter and bring her home. He saw no reason to trust the erratic nature of a train and felt somehow that his presence would correct its age-old tendency to leave the rails or to be caught beneath a Thanksgiving snow slide.

Four years at a small women's college molded Arvilla Blount permanently into what she had only tentatively been before. Her innate gentleness she came to recognize as a defect. During her first years as a first-grade teacher in a progressive private school in White Plains she learned to cover it with a protective coating of physical energy and untiring activity. She acquired all her pedagogical theory in the years in which the long shadow of John Dewey lay over the schoolrooms of the nation. For her it was a comforting philosophy. It required no hard, driving, tiring intellectual prodding of the students and herself. Instead she leaned comfortably upon such concepts as "compassion," "the peer group," "the many ages of the young," "the unblemished psyche" and "understanding the traumatized child." All of these lay within her mental grasp, she did well, even going so far as to write for the *Elementary School Journal*, in her vague but persuasive style which the editor corrected grammatically and then accepted, two articles on the profitable uses—in reading "experiences" and "social studies"—of the trips she had taken to the city with her country-raised pupils.

In all this time her uncertain grasp of the principles of agreement of pronouns with their antecedents had not improved.

Many a literate pupil of hers was startled to learn later in high school that "everyone take their book into study hall" was incorrect, because in his mind's ear he could still hear the compassionate voice of Miss Blount daily advising everyone to take their sweaters out to recess. But her voice, already colored by the fashionable accent at college, now took on the conscious, cultured tones of the parents of her pupils and of her fellow teachers. Beneath the weight of these most acceptable sounds, her grammatical solecisms seemed to be less noticeable.

When the invitation came to be Headmistress at Miss Hands, Arvilla Blount humbly felt unfit and told the visiting representatives of the Board of Governors so. But they had read her two articles, they noted with approval her maturely graying hair, her well-cut features and commanding height, the energetic way she moved blocks and small chairs to make room for them to be seated in her classroom during the interview. One of them, a former professor in Burlington, had known of her father and felt a certain security in her solid, basic Protestantism. Furthermore, she was unmarried and they liked that. They could expect her undeviating loyalty and devotion to Miss Hands. They offered her a lower starting salary than they had expected to have to pay, and in her humility she accepted at once.

Self-doubt had come later. Never again after she left her second-graders had she felt entirely secure. To save herself she moved her astonishing physical reserves to her aid, like a general whose fine plan on paper has failed and who falls back on wave after wave of men to disguise the weakness of his original strategy. Now she spent much time striding through the building of the school, like a broken stick-figure, her ravished gray face always somewhat ahead of her long, scuffed shoes, inspecting rooms for lights left burning after the occupants had gone, adjusting blinds to allow for a maximum utilization of daylight, moving chairs in preparation for the parents' arrival on the week end designated for their inspection tour, and returning chairs to their places when the visitors had departed. Her visits to classrooms, which were entered in her daybook as checks

upon the academic progress of the students and the methodology
of her teachers, were usually terminated as she reached the
thermostat at the back of the room. Acknowledging the courtesy
of the students who rose as she entered, she would pause
briefly, reach up to lower the dial on the thermostat a few degrees, listen a few moments, nod pleasantly to the teacher and
depart quietly.

For twenty years, during which the Governors (all men who
equated serenity and lack of financial problems with educational
progress) had no reason to regret their choice, she had held
her position unchallenged. She determinedly attended every
function of the school's life. If Miss Rankin, her assistant, performed all the real administrative chores within the school, she
was its ambassador-at-large, the faculty's sole representative to
the Fathers' Council, the Mothers' Club, and the Board of
Governors. To make certain that her position was never threatened by the presence of a substitute, she was never ill, and
had never been known to miss a meeting of any sort at any
time. The Governors and the parents never saw the true intellectual landscape of Miss Hands except through the compassionate optimism of Miss Blount's aging eyes, and if certain
doubts sometimes entered their minds as they listened to her
muddled and grammatically confused accounts of what was going on in the classrooms of the school, they were at once
reassured by her presentation of the year's financial statement
which she managed, by dint of small economies and even
smaller salaries (including her own), to keep always in the
black. Now, when her energies at last had diminished, her
lanky dowdiness and heavily lined face still suggested to the
Governors the capable lady they thought she had once been,
and in memory of that they respected what was left.

Having found and inspected her shoe (the day she had stood
behind the lectern at Chapel in one blue and one brown shoe
had been a severe blow to her concept of herself as a well-
kept, well-ordered lady. In that moment, seeing the amused
stares on the faces of the seniors who traditionally occupied

the front row, aware of the whispers from the lower classes, she had had a vivid memory of an old lady she had seen as a child, waiting for a streetcar on a cold Burlington street corner in a heavy, patterned bathrobe and carpet slippers), she dusted the shoe on the edge of the spread, stood up to put her foot into it, and felt for her hair.

At eight o'clock (the carillon had just sounded) it was too late to do very much about that. The thin, gray wisps, wiry and individualistic, fell downward from their usual arrangement over her ears, eternally warring with her worried fingers. Combed once at the beginning of the day, the Headmistress was never again able to pull herself into the organization of energies that was required to renew this state. Obscurely she felt that a thing done once should last, and she extended this conviction to all aspects of school life and the physical world of objects. It always seemed incomprehensible to her that in late February Miss Miers should send in an urgent request for charcoal pencils, pastel paper and beaverboard. "I distinctly remember an order for some of these things in early September," she would say to the art teacher in her high, patient voice, its tones always rendered even higher by a request that might involve money. Or again, the breakdown of the twenty-five-year-old set of refrigerators in the kitchen she attributed always to careless usage. Once she had brought herself to the violation of her financial principles that a large purchase represented, she regarded it as a permanent and eternal commitment never to be renewed. Millicent, her psychotic, swimming, blue washwoman's eyes crossing as she confronted the Headmistress with the news that the Buttery floor was filled with water from the ice-cream freezer, would be startled into silence (it was usually much easier for her to talk in her mindless, rambling way than to keep still) by the Headmistress's reminder: "But Millicent, it *can't* be broken. It's worked well all year. We've *never* had trouble with it before."

As a child in Burlington the Headmistress had learned from her father the rules for ladylike appearance, repeated them con-

scientiously to her girls and, often slyly, to those members of
the faculty who lounged about the Faculty House in Bermuda
shorts, or who ventured into eye shadow in the evenings. More
than once she had overheard Madame Mifflin: "Ladies are
aware of their *person*," shrieked the French Mistress during
those moments in class when her mission as a Lady-by-Ex-
ample seemed to her more pressing than the uses of the sub-
junctive in French, "and find discreet excuses for rectifying it
when necessary, *n'est-ce pas*, yes?" Now the Headmistress's fingers substituted for the comb she had laid down and could
not find again, they ordered some pieces behind others, tucked
strays into the fold, combined and patted as if to commend
with gentle strokes the ones that stayed where they had been
tucked.

The Headmistress had a passionate desire for order. Incapable of any real effort toward organization, she still clung to the
concept. She made lists of matters that must be attended to at
once, later in the day, that evening. She even went so far as
to have the printer for the school publication make her a
number of small pads of white paper which were headed Things
To Do Today, in This Order. At the same time she made clear
to him that she regarded the pads as due the school in the
light of her grant of the contract to him each year. But rarely
could she find the list until days later when she went through
papers on her desk. There it would be, tucked perhaps under her
bowl of African violets that drooped beside the office telephone.
But the existence of the pads contributed to her sense that
she was orderly, that the school ran well because of this *sense*
of order, even if little she did was within its bounds.

Again she tucked. She knew the habit exasperated her assistant, Miss Rankin, who always lost her train of thought at
the sight of the groping, sightless fingers at work among the
wisps of gray hair. But the Headmistress was powerless before
her need to appear, to her fingers at least, well-groomed and in
order.

She turned away from the mirror, where she had stopped to

check the results, and gave her room a last, satisfied look. Slightly larger than the other rooms on the floor, it emanated an air of scholarship. Piles of reports from the National Association of Principals were stacked on a straight-backed chair. A paper-covered Conant Report, the controversial Rickover book, its cover pristine, and a severe-looking, block-printed cover to a volume call *Education in the Age of Science* were piled on a table intended for plants which stood beside the easy chair. Clearly arranged for evening and leisure-time reading, the books were meant to suggest to the visitor a deep professional concern with the pressing problems of modern education. But to the Headmistress, deep in her unacknowledged conscience, and beneath the picture of herself she wished her room to suggest to a casual passer-by, the books wistfully represented the unattainable. Her social self was afraid of being alone long enough to read. It would make her linger in the sitting room in the evenings until her eyelids grew heavy. Then, later, in her room, stretched out in her chair with the Conant Report or *Education in the Age of Science* she would fall asleep after the first or second scholarly sentence. Her quotations from these works, which customarily introduced little speeches to the Board of Governors or friendly opening remarks to Faculty meetings, came from typed summaries made by Miss Rankin from library copies of the works: having suggested the books to Miss Rankin as "excellent" or "stimulating," the Headmistress came to feel she had done the books entire justice, and that the quotes Miss Rankin found and copied out for her were really at her direction.

Her desk was obscured by manila folders, reverently dusted and stacked by Millicent's younger sister, Rita, who "did up" the Faculty House. To Rita's flat, foolish hand these folders seemed to encase all of human learning, and the care with which she handled them each day communicated itself to the Headmistress who as a result saw in them another legitimate facet of her intellectual life. Each folder bore the label: *Articles to be Read*. From their edges protruded narrow columns of newsprint: the Headmistress spent an hour every Sunday evening, as the rest of the faculty chattered around her in the sitting room, clipping what appeared to her to be pertinent articles from the *Times*, articles she felt certain would provide her with matter for chapel talks and faculty reports on *New Trends in Curriculum Planning*. Having filed them away in their manila folders (the presence of the word "student" or "education" or "teacher" in their titles made them eligible for inclusion) the urgency to read them deserted her. The act of separating them from the other newspaper irrelevancies constituted an entirely adequate substitute for further exploration.

She stooped to pick up yesterday's *Times* lying where she had dropped it at the side of her bed last evening. It was open to the page of engagement announcements. Always in these last minutes before sleep when she felt it necessary to provide against the nightly ax of conscience (*why haven't I done something about Sophie Seward, why did I let Rankin correct me in front of the seniors about the order of march for Commencement, why is Ellen Acton after all these years still so determinedly insolent, when will the seniors decide on their flowers, when, why, why*) and her ineluctable sense of inadequacy, she would search the announcements for some saving sign of success, some mention of a girl who had passed through Miss Hands and who had arrived at a place of prominence in the public prints. Obscurely she was comforted when she found a name she knew, almost provided for against the multitudinous rebuffs dealt her by the Ellen Actons and the sharp, ambitious, frightening intelligence of Miss Rankin.

Clutching the *Times* under her arm, the Headmistress went out. She shut the door with great restraint behind her, not so much in an effort to maintain the still sleeping faculty in their laggard state as to serve as a model of correct deportment. Jo Long, coming out of the bathroom in an immaculate sweat shirt and long-legged sweat pants in which she always slept, smiled and excused herself, flattening against the wall to let her pass.

"Good morning, Miss Blount." Jo's voice was high and joyous, and rang with the firmness of a born field-hockey umpire.

"Good morning, Miss Long," said the Headmistress as she passed, smiled quickly and went down the stairs. The Headmistress was scrupulous about maintaining the fiction of professional address. She had known and lived in the same House with Jo Long for seven years, she had been witness to all the horrifying privacies and intimacies that women expose to each other in such mutual living, but she had never addressed her by her first name, and she never would.

Still holding the *Times* open to the announcement of Eleanor Ames's engagement in Bridgeport ("she was a graduate of Miss Hands School for Girls and Bennett Junior College, a provisional member of the Bridgeport Junior League") the Headmistress went into the sitting room. She gave the room, now lightened by May morning sun, a comprehensive glance. It had been noted more than once by Roberta Parks, who hated order and lived in a happy state of mess which gave her a deceptive sense of the richness of life, that the Headmistress had the soul of an upstairs maid. At odd moments of the day, when the waiting room held a visitor patiently reading old copies of *The Writing Hand,* and her secretary hovered about waiting for her to sign checks, Miss Blount might be found straightening the rows of chairs in the auditorium, whose haphazard seating arrangement after the students had nudged their way through always offended her, or picking gum wrappers out of the myrtle patch under her office window.

Now she picked up Ellen's abandoned coffee cup. Balancing it grimly on top of the *Times,* she carried it into the backstairs landing where a stove, vintage icebox and a cupboard, in the top of which a small porcelain sink was embedded, served as a makeshift kitchen. The Headmistress had never been eager to encourage cooking in Faculty House, feeling that such activity somehow would serve as criticism of the quality and volume of the food regularly served in the Buttery. So these three roomless objects were a silent reminder to faculty members who wanted to avoid the rituals, the warmed leftovers and the forced camaraderie of Buttery meals that this was *not* a kitchen but a motley assemblage of unmatched appliances without specific uses.

The Headmistress stood the cup and saucer on the stove but made no move to wash them, hoping that the mere act of transferring them from sitting room to stove would serve as some sort of check upon Miss Acton's slovenly Irish habits. Momentarily distracted again, she stood at the stove and read the article about Eleanor Ames, now Mrs. Calvin Shumacher III ("he is a graduate of the Choate School and Princeton University, where he was a member of The Tower Club . . ."). The carillon rang eight-thirty, the Headmistress pushed the front portion of her hair back under the heavier levels of back hair, ripped the article she had been reading from the paper, and walked rapidly to the front door. She dropped the remains of the paper on the front-hall table, its violated side placed carefully down, satisfying her yearning for order. She went out into the oppressive May morning, her gray head bent against the heat, the back hem of her dress dipping gently toward the grass-lined path.

Lying motionless in her bed in Elias Cook House, her yellow hair wetted down by a bottomless grief of her adolescent sleep, Trudy Langer heard the eight-thirty carillon, and turned her face to the rose-sprinkled wall. She had been dreaming of things she had never known, of the mysterious culminations of sex, of love in the shape of primitive African figurines. Twice, earlier, she had awakened to throw off the horror of her dreams, and gone back to sleep. Now, as the carillon broke in upon her first sound sleep of the night, she could not wholly surrender to wakefulness.

A Saturday. Only this thought could rouse her, and slowly it moved into the yellow area between her lids and her eyes. She forced them open. *No classes. No uniform. No damned*

Rankin the Fox watching me from every window and every door, with her eight pairs of eyes, all red. Reynard the Rankin. Luxuriating in the absence of so many weekday irritants, Trudy turned on her back and settled herself comfortably to ignore the carillon. Then suddenly, as if propelled by something within the mattress, she sat up, swung her bare legs over the side of the bed, and pushed her wet hair back out of her eyes. Her roommate Johanna was gone. This was not a blessed, free, magnificent Saturday. *This is the day the Disciplinary Committee meets, the vicious, pernicious damnable Disciplinary Committee, which will louse up this whole week end and probably next week end too, restricting me to campus, or that other hell, supervised Study Halls after dinner for a week, or no extra-curricular activity until Commencement. That dope Seward will be there complaining, sweating, full of evidence, her degraded aristocratic beak pointing at me, her hands shaking, the pure and lovely victim of my nastiness. Volpone Rankin, lord of the flies, secretary of the Committee, chairman of everything else in this damned neck of the woods, Pooh-Ba Lord High Everything Else, will shriek rules and manners, and Miss Blount, the white sheep, the Little Shepherd of the Hills, will say, in her "I love them all" high voice, "You didn't mean to do it, did you, Trudy dear?" God damn the whole blasted, tree-lined, ivy-coated place. God damn Jamie Roebling most of all. I did mean to do it.*

Jamie Roebling was Trudy Langer's secret love. She believed in love, like all the other girls on her floor and of her age. Her faith rested upon ignorance, and she acted upon it as if it were axiomatic. Love was real, and love waited just outside the gates of Miss Hands, fulsome and glowing and newly adorned with Mennen, a full alligator wallet and shined shoes, full of laughing talk, waiting beside a ticking taxi. Love would rush to hold the door; love would rescue her from boredom and from the Big Sister eyes of Miss Rankin. Like most of the other seniors at Miss Hands Trudy talked graphically of experiences she had never had. Her few, brief encounters with men, limited to heavily chaperoned dances with the boys from St. Martin's, had given her only vague intimations of the truth. The rest she and the others in rooms in her corridor had been forced, during impromptu sessions, to fabricate. Seldom did their stories of high sexual adventure descend into detail, never did they approach the grimy face of realism, such as the girls had beheld in surreptitiously obtained copies of Erskine Caldwell, Henry Miller and D. H. Lawrence. More often they would return from spring recess with legends, tales that resembled in spirit the quest for the Holy Grail, the *Romance of the Rose*, whole cycles of allegories which were merely elaborations upon a date for the movies with a boy who lived down the street and went to State.

Only the actual existence of Jamie Roebling supplied a touch of realism to Trudy's dreams. He was major of St. Martin's battalion. He had, by the end of his junior year, acquired all the prizes offered by the military and academic faculties. Once, at the Christmas Formal, he had asked Trudy to dance.

About this core of fact Trudy had erected a soul-satisfying fiction. Jamie would call her (although in some of her narrations to her friends he had already done so and had been summarily refused), ask her to the Military Ball in May, and then somewhere (Harvard and Radcliffe? Columbia and Barnard?): "Why you're Trudy Langer, that lovely girl I danced with at Miss Hands last year! Like a cup of coffee? Or a beer? Yes, much better, a beer. I know a place out on the State Road. My car's right here. The red convertible. 'Let us go, you and I, when the evening is spread out against the sky. . . .'"

Trudy saw no practical obstacles to the fulfillment of her dream. Her lank yellow hair which started far back on her forehead in its retreat down her waist, her over-white skin which announced anxiety, fear and rising embarrassment with a scurf of blotches, a burning nose, and irritated skin, her eyes which were constantly red-rimmed with staring into the future: she knew all this to be unbeautiful, but she believed that Jamie, blinded by a true inner vision of her need, would see none of it.

In her deeper self she acknowledged a greater barrier to his ultimate recognition of her: he was Educated, and she, despite the elevated prose-promises in Miss Hands's *Bulletin:*

> *The girls at Miss Hands receive a thorough and sensitive grounding in all the elements of the English Language, and in the last two years of their high school life they are introduced to, and made deeply acquainted with, the whole panoramic history of English Literature. There will be parallel excursions into American Literature whenever it seems feasible, to illustrate the trends and influences shared by the two cultures.*

had been exposed to much important subject matter without any appreciable effect. She had sat through Physics (*Every graduate of Miss Hands will have had a year of Modern Physics*) and Latin Three, dissected smelts in Biology, and sought out, with Miss Parks who far preferred it to Caesar, the original of Catullus' *Lesbia*, but she had understood very little of what she was doing, and cared less. She had, at Miss Rankin's insistence, applied for entry to three colleges, and had not heard from any of them. To her mind learning now had the patina of punishment ("Go read a book," her young, divorced mother had often said to her when she was expecting a guest, or when the very sight of the anguished face of her over-tall adolescent daughter irritated her). She felt she had somehow failed to take a proper position during her parents' divorce and that now she was paying the price for her mistake by attendance at Miss Hands. No one, she felt, could fail to suspect her genuine ignorance, her lifelong stupidity, her lack of understanding of every subject to which she had been submitted. Only to her own deep hungers was she truly educated. Before Jamie's piercing eyes Trudy felt naked and hopeless.

Now, as she sat upon the edge of her bed, the day for her had darkened. From the corners of her room a cloud moved in, covering her earlier feelings of Saturday freedom. She started to dress, stopped to search through her laundry bag for a pair of jeans, twisted off a button on her boy's shirt as she tried to push it into its hole, and thrust down viciously to jam her shirt tails into the top of her jeans. With one angry motion she caught at her hair, blindly wrapped a rubber band around it close to her head and let the rest hang, tangled and uncombed, almost to her waist. Ignoring her towel and toothbrush, she took up the hymnal from her desk, and banged the door shut behind her. The floor of Elias Cook Hall shook as she pounded her sneakered, furious feet down toward the stairs.

At the bulletin board on the landing Emily Courtney and Ruthie Vandermeer were reading a pinned-up clipping.

Ruthie intoned: "She spent a year at the Sorbonne following her graduation from Bennett Junior College. She . . ."

"Who's the new, proud, engaged daughter of the Firm Hand?" asked Trudy.

"A success," said Emily, who was tall, dark-skinned and much admired for her American-Indian features. She thought highly of Trudy's rebellious spirit without having the courage to emulate it. "Remember Ames? We were freshmen when she was here. She played basketball, I think. Not only engaged, though. About to marry someone in Bridgeport."

"That drip. Bully for her," said Trudy without stopping. As she pounded down the stairs, she retreated instinctively, habitually, to a world of her own composition: *Gertrude Mead Langer, girl senior, spent four remorseless years at Miss Hands School for Comfortable Daughters of Nastily Divorced Parents. She is a member of the Provisional League of Rebels Against all Restraining Forces Whatever. Her clubs are all secret, including The Scurvy Elephants. She regularly attends the Black Mass, and is in constant demand at the biweekly sessions of the Disciplinary Committee.*

Trudy went out the front door, slamming it hard behind her. The windows rattled. As an afterthought she kicked at the shaky porch railing before she started across the Quad lawn, sending two slumbering ladybugs aloft in panic.

Jo Long turned back from the window. The air outside seemed warmer than the lingering night air inside, so she had closed Robbie's window gently, watching Trudy Langer storm out of Elias Cook toward the Buttery, and knowing how Robbie hated to be awakened by loud noises.

"Arise, my love," she said, pulling back the sheets Robbie always held around her like a winding sheet. She poked Robbie's shoulder gently with her fist.

"Go away, watchman. This is Saturday."

"Oh yes, oh yes, it is. Saturday. But a special Saturday, the *last* Saturday. Final-meetings Saturday. Plans for soft-parent-soap Saturday and hard-detergent-disciplinary committee meetings for me Saturday. *And* Chapel."

"Chapel? Saturday? *Hostis humani generis.*"

"Pretty good for eight o'clock. Care to parse a bit of Catullus?"

Roberta Parks had learned her Latin at a girls' preparatory school in Maine and then at Radcliffe. Raised by two maiden aunts whom she frightened from the time she could walk by her erratic displays of energy and unexpected outbursts of physical violence which often turned back upon herself, she was sent away to school at twelve. Eagerly, as each vacation period approached, the aunts awaited her return, baked brownies, aired her room which was larger and lighter than the one they shared. Their delight at the sight of their sun-tanned niece was usually cut short almost at once. She was a sullen, introverted girl whose dead silences began ten minutes after she caught sight of her aunts. They would not have believed the pathetically eager-to-please roommate at the Academy or, later, the quietly intent member of the fencing squad at Radcliffe to be the wordless niece upstairs reading. Robbie never questioned this metamorphosis in herself, but she recognized its existence and went home less and less. The aunts Parks grew feeble. With their terminal energies they found their two pictures of Roberta in her graduation cap and gown (white from the Academy, black from college) more consoling and gentler than the presence of the girl herself. Her pictures stood beside those of her dead parents, the double old-gold frame beside the uniformed portrait of their brother, a stern captain in his high khaki collar, and his wife, whom the aunts had always called Miss Avery, a Southern girl who had died of meningitis six months after Roberta's birth. Out of her dual self on the mantel Roberta smiled uncharacteristically at them, and they were once more quietly pleased. They grew feebler as they sat among their portraits, rarely visited, sustaining each other with fictions about their brilliant and loving niece. Aunt Elizabeth Parks died at eighty-four from a fall down the heady front steps of her Maine house. Roberta came home for the funeral and stayed only long enough to settle Aunt Jane into a Portland nursing home.

"Be a good girl," she said in her deep, boyish voice to the frail old woman who clung to her in the new home. Robbie hated scenes and feared even more displays of emotion that were aimed at her. They made her surly and brisk with the sufferer and harsh with anyone who looked to her for reassurance.

"I will try, Roberta. Do come to see me when you can."

Robbie nodded, turned away and never saw Aunt Jane alive again. Working for her master's degree in education she lived in a small, airless room in Cambridge which she filled with books, elegant boys' shirts and dark-plaid Bermudas. For the rest of her life large bedrooms were to depress her and make her feel empty and imposed upon, as if something too much was being expected of her. She rarely wore a skirt, spent what little money the sale of the house brought her on anatomical reproductions of sculpture by Zorach and Epstein, good reprints of Picasso's circus families and rope belts for her jeans and clam diggers. She bicycled around Cambridge, from Harvard to her rooming house, she read Christopher Isherwood, André Gide and Baudelaire, she explored bookstores and art cinemas, always glad of company but never afraid of being alone. Something about her sullen jaw and harshly cut hair discouraged girlish confidences and shows of grief from the graduate students in her house, and only by chance did she come upon another human being to share her separation.

Josephine Long came from a vast, sprawling, cheerful family. Her love for Robbie was merely an extension into sexual passion of what had been lifelong, generous, familial affection. The Longs lived in a large nineteenth-century house in Minneapolis. Doctor Long considered that his nine tumbling, shouting children gave to the house, in which he also practiced, an air of prosperity. Even without patients the house looked busy. This air of activity and success relaxed and reassured the general practitioner to the point where it was often difficult to make him go out on calls or to leave the jovial good humor of prolonged family dinners to see patients downstairs in his basement dispensary. Jo's life with her sisters was comradely, but her truest alliances were with her brothers who recognized the odd streak of steel and unfeminine reticence in her character and accepted her as one of them.

At the University of Michigan, where she went on a scholarship awarded as much to the feckless doctor's bookkeeping ineptitude and his number of other children as to her middling high-school record, Jo was lonely and homesick. In intramural girls' basketball however, she found a sustaining substitute for the comradeship of back-yard basketball. Her teammates were satisfying replicas of her brothers. She admired the girls' devotion to each other at moments of struggle on the court, their warm unity in defeat, their open-armed, uncontrolled ecstasy when they won. In the locker room after a game, a warm shower, and dressed in clean white shirts and shorts, she found the same charm about their slim, bared sunburned arms and long legs that she had loved in her brothers, and her fraternal affections turned irrevocably to a love of women.

Standing under the foundress's disjointed finger on the first evening of her third year of teaching History at Miss Hands, Jo saw Roberta Parks standing alone in a corner drinking coffee. The electric light of the converted gas lamps made Robbie's arms appear burned and muscular. Her lower jaw, set hard,

seemed posed against the assembled chattering faculty, reunited
after a long summer recess from their usual intimacies.

Jo crossed the long room, avoiding the central mahogany
table with a nimble jerk of her hips. To Robbie, who watched
her approach, she was like a solitary forward avoiding the grasp-
ing arms of the opposition's guard. Her hair was damp, and
curled about her ears.

"Are you new?"

"I am." The blunt tone of Robbie's reply discouraged Jo's
natural delight in talk, but only for a moment.

Still, there was something . . .

"English?" Jo asked, tentatively.

"No, Latin."

This was enough. Jo set off again in her fast, happy way,
her talk rattling down a familiar track.

"Oh yes, you must be Mrs. Stafford's replacement. She
was sort of an old fool, but nice. Dramatized everything. Ora-
tions, Roman dinners, stretched out on her desk. Her son died
last year. A Harvard fellow. Hanged himself in the men's room
of Dunster Hall. Took the starch out of old Staff. I think she's a
house mother at Skidmore this year."

"Was she a good Latin teacher?"

"The girls loved her. She let them do pretty much as they
pleased."

"I doubt they'll like me much then."

Jo looked at Robbie's jaw that had loosened and softened
as she talked.

"Have you been to your room yet?"

"Yes. Third floor in the rear. Or at least I think it's rear.
It was dark when I came."

"Next to mine if it's Staff's old one."

"Probably."

Together they walked back to the coffee urn, separating only
to pass the massive center table. Refilling their coffee under
Miss Hands's indicative finger they contracted their silent pact.
In the years that followed, despite wounding, almost mortal

quarrels in which they told corrosive truths to each other, the
sullen Robbie Parks and the undaunted, gay Jo Long became
one. Alone in their separate classrooms, sitting apart but watching each other at faculty meals, they were one in their evenings
and in their early mornings, one in the single, total joy their
perversely unified sex represented. Neither suffered from any
sense of deprivation of the normal, the customary, the socially
acceptable. Rather, they felt above and beyond the others in
their House, in their one, vital sense, sufficient to themselves
and to each other but now most blessedly without the old
needs that had plagued them both all their singular lives. They
never realized that the students called them "The Twins"; if
they had, they would have found no real objection to the satiric
title.

It was hot in Robbie's room. Jo felt uncomfortable in her
sweat shirt and pants, and still damp from her shower. Her
hair, wet from its morning washing (Robbie never bothered to
hide her scorn at Jo's unshakable conviction that she must
wash her hair twice a day) was beginning to curl in the heat.
She opened the window again and walked to the door. As she
passed Robbie's bed she leaned over.

"I'm leaving now. I've got to dress. Are you really awake?"

"Um."

"Sure?" Jo stroked Robbie's back in comradely fashion and
then, in a sudden rush of feeling, bent over and kissed her.

"See you at breakfast. I want to ask you about something
when you're really awake. Don't forget there's Chapel."

"*Quand même*," mumbled Robbie, but Jo had already closed
the door.

Robbie lay still, bathed in the warmth of her bed, in the air
that blew in from the already steaming lawns, furious at Jo's
last words. *I know what she wants, to ask me if she can invite
Sophie Seward to the cabin. Sophie the poor, Sophie the weak,
Sophie the lily maid. . . .* Oppressed by the heat of her objections, Robbie crashed out of bed and dropped her pajama
top on the floor. She looked at her spare body in the mirror

above the bare bureau, at her narrow body, at her breasts that lay, solid and small, against her chest like afterthoughts imposed upon a male figure, at her short, carefully waved brown hair, a camouflage against the truth about her and Jo. As she dressed she steeled herself to resistance. *Jo's weak when it comes to spewing sympathy around for all the world's delicate children. I won't have that squid Sophie ruining the first free month we've had since last August. To hell with Jo's damned Methodist charity. She can save it for church. . . .*

Madame Madeleine Mifflin taught French. Her room, from which, at the sound of the eight-thirty carillon, delighting in her promptness, she habitually emerged, was arranged in what she regarded as purely French fashion. Two high-back chairs were painted black with hand-gilded floral designs on the back rests. The walls on the two sides where there were no mirrors were covered with travel posters, her bed was draped with a tapestry-like spread, the little shelf of paperback French novels was held erect between two empty Chianti bottles, their straw raveling gently down the black and gold front of her battered *commode*, imported from Grand Rapids. Madame's passion for France was all the stronger because she had not been in her native Bordeaux since her departure as a girl of seventeen. More French in speech and dress than the Junior French mistress, Mademoiselle Loivin, whose first year away from Paris was just ending, it seemed that geographic closeness to the roots of her consciousness was unnecessary to Madame (whom the girls in all innocence always called "Madam"). Only her accent had suffered during her long exile from her homeland. As she felt it slipping she substituted safeguards against its total disappearance. These were French-sounding barriers against Anglicized speech, little phonetic clucks and exclamations which she felt preserved the liquid tones of her speech from the barbaric cacophony of the language around her.

Against Ellen Acton she directed the full force of her nationalism. Miss Acton had a number of times in her classes suggested the heresy that all western culture, literary movements of note, original musical concepts and architectural trends did not originate in France. Miss Acton never mentioned Madame Mifflin's misconceptions in her lectures on, for example, the English metaphysical poets, but the specter of the passionate, compact little Frenchwoman hovered over the heads of the listening students, almost at the threshhold of the English Room. At dinner that evening Ellen could expect an attack on her point of view, which surely had reached Madame. Ruthie Vandermeer took both English and French Four, and was ambitious.

Madame was stout and solid and short. Dark, brisk hair trailed from her head and her black, somehow very French eyes would pin her listener to the wall as she unblinkingly demanded an audience for her latest description of an American horror she had heard or read about, some catastrophe which could not have happened under the French way of life, a violation of human sensibilities that French culture would have prevented. Her voice was sharp and vicious, and her way with English words was to imbue them with the mystery of foreignness that came from a heavy application of her accent to the most commonplace substantives and conjunctions, thus adding a mysterious authority to their lowly grammatical stature and a subtlety to all commonplace observations.

Madame had been married, many years ago, to a ne'er-do-well American ornithologist. Against her deepest religious convictions, which she brought with her untouched and untried from a convent school in Bordeaux, she had allowed herself to form an alliance with Stephen Lucas whom she secretly regarded as dangerously heretical in his New England Methodism and without any of the prerequisite Gallic sensibilities. When he had suffered long enough under her point of view and felt it was hopeless ever to gain a common acceptance from her, he disappeared without notice into the mists of east Europe while on a solitary scholarly visit, soon after their tenth wedding anniversary. Madame's reaction had been practical, decisive.

She tucked his name, slightly Europeanized, behind her maiden name, separated only by an aristocratic hyphen, sold their few belongings, and in a month was settled, as the widowed Mme. Lukacs-Mifflin, a teacher of conversational French, at the Crestwood School for Girls in Palo Alto. Within herself she regarded her marriage as proof of a correct and orderly approach to life by a proper Frenchwoman. When it had been disordered by Stephen Lucas's disappearance she had made all the appropriate changes. Only one of her acts of adjustment was to puzzle her in her more introspective moments: on the day she learned of her husband's defection, she left the Roman Catholic Church and in time became an active Methodist. It was as if her staunch defense of her faith, which had withstood his presence, crumbled at the moment he was no longer there to challenge it. Now a vigorous Protestant, she taught Sunday School in whatever town she lived in or near, and read pointedly from the Revised Standard Version of the Bible. Before falling asleep she would murmur an almost apologetic Hail Mary, hastily cross herself, and settle the pillow for the night.

After a year at Crestwood she moved to another girls' school, and in the years since her "loss," as she called Stephen, she made her way slowly eastward, little by little acquiring an air of exile, fortifying her accent, and speaking often and in every possible connection of her children now at school in Switzerland, at "French schools there, of course." To parents of her students she seemed a pathetic but gallant emigrée, whose solid little French body seemed anachronistic beside the straight back, the short hair, the rigorous American body, the long, narrow capable feet of Miss Moore, the gym teacher, for example. While acknowledging her warm sympathy for the affairs of others, the rest of the faculty feared Madame's tongue, her patriotic diatribes, but most of all her long, involuted and constant references to the diurnal affairs of her son and her daughter.

Today her face bore the marks of determined sympathy. She had gone to bed with the disturbing memory of last evening's nastiness. Returned to the sitting room after the Senior

Final Show, the faculty had stood up to drink its late instant coffee. Talk had started with the Headmistress.

"It was a very nice show, Miss Seward."

Madame spoke at once.

"I found the English hard. I think Shakespeare is trying for a European, do not you?" Madame's remark was meant to be kind, to cover the bare fact that none of the girls had been able to memorize the difficult iambic pentameter of *The Merchant of Venice,* and that a few of them, inspired by long-standing, well-developed scorn of Miss Seward, had purposely sabotaged the production.

"There was very little time to rehearse," Sophie Seward said, almost inaudibly. The Headmistress decided to cover this remark quickly, implying as it did some criticism of her assistant Elizabeth Rankin's scheduling of the events of the past two weeks. She said quickly:

"It's good to expose the girls to great works." Her hand reached furtively for stray hairs and tucked them back, making a patchwork pattern, blindly, of the back of her head. Miss Rankin, standing alone near the door, stared at the Headmistress, frowned, and said nothing. Jo and Robbie smiled at each other. The Headmistress saw them, and felt compelled to go on.

"Under the circumstances I thought they did quite well, didn't you, Miss Acton?"

Ellen hesitated, considered. The Headmistress, in the darkened back rows of the auditorium, had probably slept fitfully during most of the performance, waking only in time to join in the polite applause. Ellen debated agreement, but could not bring herself to it. As Senior English Mistress her job for the play had been limited to pulling the curtains. From this vantage point she had watched the girls reading their lines from ragged copies of the play pinned to their hats, to their cloaks, to the stage furniture. Now she was hot, it was late, she was tired.

She said: "I think it's better to do no play at all than to put on something serious that the girls make fun of all through."

There was silence. Jo went on smiling, this time in embarrassment at the floor.

Sophie repeated miserably, "We rehearsed only in class
periods, and some of these were taken to be used for testing."

Everyone sensed trouble. Madame Mifflin said hastily, "I
thought Vandermeer was charming in that *Second Shepherd's
Play* cloak." Jo Long stopped smiling at the floor, and looked
surreptitiously at Miss Rankin. Ellen murmured to Lucy Moore,
at the same time that Madame spoke: "That's tore it," but no
one else heard. Meg Miers, sketching the back of Robbie's
head on the end pages of her spiral class roll, said, to no one
in particular, "Take a window." Everyone waited, like fore-
warned coastal dwellers who have received storm warnings of
coming violence.

Miss Rankin's furies were dreaded. Needing no elaborate
kindling and no match, they leaped up without warning. She
was as much feared because her emotions lay so close to the
surface as because of the instantaneous conflagration she often
started among sensitive members of the faculty. It was as if
prediction about Miss Rankin was impossible. Hiding her motives and disguising her reactions to those around her, no one
knew her well enough to foresee either her fury or her close-
to-tears silences. Both were equally ominous. Her voice, like
the subcutaneous color that rushed up her knotted neck to her
chin and lips, reacted in an instant. Within the space of a short
sentence, with the unbelievable virtuosity of a great soprano,
it would ascend to a shrill, threatening plane. Before it, and
the unearthly sound it attained, the whole faculty retreated as
before the approaching whine of an artillery shell.

When she spoke, the threatened storm broke.

"It's impossible to schedule an over-ambitious thing like this
successfully. I remember clearly pointing this out at the last
faculty meeting. No one has the least idea"—her voice started
its Himalayan rise—"of how complicated a thing the schedule is.
Everyone wants rehearsals, special classes, extra events, and I

am left with it and all the *essential* testing as well, and seven periods a day to fit it all into."

Miss Rankin's long, harshly boned face shone with passion. Her gray hair, pulled back tight from her forehead, seemed to be all that was left to bind in the hysteria that rattled from the tones of her voice and flickered behind her eyelids.

"Quite right," said the Headmistress, growing anxious and feeling too sleepy to handle the crisis. Her reliance upon Miss Rankin was absolute, almost desperate. Knowing how tenuous was her own grasp of the realities of the whole educational process, how confused matters of immediate decision became when, under pressure, she took matters into her own hands, she used what energies were still hers to protect Miss Rankin. She was an anxious, feeble monarch hovering over the kingdom's strongest hero, threatened by self-doubts, but not wishing to abdicate.

"Anything else?"

Sophie, knowing better, still could not prevent herself from speaking. She had gathered what was left of her lost case for a last desperate appeal. The futility of it colored her voice.

"Miss Blount, it was not really so ambitious. At the Millbrook School a few years ago that play went very well, or so many people said to me afterwards. Parents said . . ."

The Headmistress's hand went to the light switch. The lights flickered twice.

"Curtain going down, ladies." She found pleasure in this reference to the theatre, as if her life were lived in its memory, or in its constant shadow.

"But here, with Trudy Langer's vicious little mind behind everything, egging the girls on to see dirty jokes behind simple words, and aping me—I could feel it behind my back. . . ."

"Miss Seward," now the Headmistress's tired defenses were alert and militant. "Miss Seward," and her voice rose slightly at the repetition, the key now suggesting the command which represented twenty years of such moments as Headmistress, *"that girl is not vicious.* She is high-strung, yes, but not vicious. You have misunderstood her utterly, as you have misunderstood other girls here this year, and in doing so you have made her even more—more nervous and tense."

Miss Blount's feverish defense of Trudy was, to Sophie, a personal assault. She saw it as a public announcement to the rest of the faculty that she had not been "asked back," and as a carefully drawn-up and posted revelation of her personal failures. The faculty recognized it, more charitably, as a general statement of the Headmistress's undeviating concept of the characters of her girls. To her, judgments concerning them were always relative. They depended on such matters as the social position of the father, the state of the family's account with the office, and the number of other female children in the family who were prospective students. In all these respects Trudy Langer qualified for the staunch support of her Headmistress as a girl of the highest integrity: her father had been lieutenant governor of Connecticut, he paid her considerable bill at the beginning of each semester with admirable promptness, she had (although unfortunately they were now living with her remarried mother) two younger sisters.

"If there is a fault, Miss Seward, it must lie in your insensitivity to her needs. She is a very troubled girl." The compassion in the Headmistress's voice was professional but real. In her inability to understand the deeper stresses of adolescents she retired to the comfort of her conviction that they were all "troubled" and that their treatment should begin with recognition of this fact. She regarded them always as needing her assurances of understanding. That no genuine understanding on her part followed these assurances did not prevent her from offering them. Like Benjamin Franklin she believed that the appearance of a virtue was often a very satisfactory substitute for the virtue itself.

Ellen Acton closed her eyes and braced herself, her hands holding the caned bottom of her chair. *Now comes the clincher, the special, bonded cliché reserved for these moments of dealing with difficult faculty matters, the good-housekeeping-seal-of-approval bromide.*

"It is always," the Headmistress said, "when they are most unlovable that they most need love."

"Amen," said Ellen under her breath, to Robbie.

"*Quand même,*" said Robbie, her eyes in mock piety on the gilt seal above the fireplace.

Sophie began to shake. Of all the evidences of stress at Miss Hands this year, Sophie's inability to control her shaking hands and head was most distressing to the other teachers. Her head would move up and down in a rapid little negation, a denial by tic of the latest assault upon her. In an effort not to drop her cup, her fingers turned white. Miss Rankin, watching her steadily, showed no elation at her own tacit victory. She put her cup down on the sideboard, and the fact that she had allowed herself to move at all, while the battle still raged, showed confidence in her position. Quietly she stepped over to the Headmistress and said something into her ear.

The Headmistress nodded.

"Oh yes, ladies. You will remember of course there is Chapel tomorrow, for the purpose of . . ."

She faltered. Miss Rankin, not looking at her and hardly moving her lips, spoke quietly to her again.

"Of rehearsing for the Parents' Arrival Procession and Commencement."

Miss Rankin nodded. The sound of Sophie's cup rattling in her saucer filled the room.

"All faculty will be present, of course, and please, without morning newspapers or other distractions. We must serve as examples to the girls. Ten o'clock."

Ellen thought: *she means me. I'll leave my breviary in my room and muffle the rattling of my beads.*

Jo thought: *clearly meant for me. Now I'll have to correct those history quizzes before I go to bed tonight.*

Mademoiselle Loivin was never sure of anyone's intent in English. She thought: *I will not read the paper where the girls can see it.*

Moving to the door, the Headmistress playfully repeated the ceremony of the blinking of the lights.

"Goodnight," she said and went out. Miss Rankin followed her at once.

The murmur of goodnight went around the room. Everyone avoided looking at Sophie as they wished her goodnight with more than their usual concern for her inclusion in the general greeting.

Robbie, the last one out, turned off the lights. "Sisters," she said to everyone at once and no one in particular, "let us adjourn to our cells."

Remembering the bitter tone of Robbie's valedictory and the general acidity of the air in the sitting room last night, Madame went down the hall, bathed in determined charity. *I will talk to that Sophie this morning.* Madame, who had written so many quizzes requiring the proper use of the demonstrative pronoun, used them always before important nouns, as if to settle in her mind their emphatic place in English. *I will find what she intends for herself this summer. Clearly she is not to return. Perhaps a dinner, perhaps a week end in the Cape near where the girls have their villa. Money perhaps. I know she is borrowing always from that Acton. I will perhaps offer her some.*

It was always a little hard for Madame to know how to channel her effusions of sympathy. The truth was that her desire to help was always in direct proportion to her need to *know*, to be privy to the secrets of those with whom she lived so that she might woo others with her exclusive disclosure of them. Sophie's plight to her was principal on which to draw. Last evening's unpleasantness was merely an added rub, a new pustule in the year-long emotional eczema that the English teacher had sustained. *I will take a seat beside her in the Chapel and speak then to her. I will speak of Jean and Dorothea. One's own troubles attract and draw out those of others. They suggest confession to others. I will offer her some of mine . . . mine and my children's.*

Madame, hopeful of gain from Sophie—*today there may be*

something—walked across the white-hot pavement toward the Buttery, stepping aside only once to make room for Lucy Moore to pass.

Out of Faculty House, three steps at a time down the front stairs, and across the first of the three diagonals that formed the pavement between the House and the Buttery, the long, handsome, bronzed gym teacher ran. She moved in slow, disciplined lopes, feeling intense joy in the regular movement of her arms. She remembered to point her chin up, to flex her foot purposely behind her at each stride. Her face was set with pleasure. She passed Madame Mifflin, nodded smiling, the slight breeze her passage created riffling the charming blonde bangs on her forehead, lifting them into the air through which she passed. Feeling keen pleasure that she was not required to stop and speak—for Lucy physical activity of any sort was infinitely less tiring than even the simplest expletive—she ran on, barely winded by the time she came to the Buttery steps. Her cheeks were glowing, she felt suffused with the pleasant warmth that invaded her body when she exerted it, and the mental warmth she always experienced when she knew she had used it well and according to all the rules she had been taught. A *lovely, lovely day*, she thought, and with a mighty, well-coordinated pull of both arms, she opened the doors to the Buttery, and bounded in.

Madame, taking lady-like, short, buttressed steps, watched Lucy run. Her youth and shining face seemed to the French Mistress an offense to her own essentially interior existence. *That all-American body*, she thought. *That, that, that . . . girl.*

Eight-thirty. Mrs. Bache locked the door of her room. She was sure the Twins romped around her room during her labs, reading her letters, disturbing her file of old biology and physics quizzes, riffling through the pages of her collection of Israeli

and World Refugee Year stamps. One evening she had found
a cigarette butt in one of the ash trays she had brought with
her from Europe, a flattened-down Tablets of the Law in mosaic
tile with tiny metal hands on two sides to hold the cigarette.
Later she remembered that "they" had been in her room during
the afternoon to borrow some soap powder. But the suspicion
had been planted once, and she completely ignored the truth
under the obscuring weight of prior suspicion.

Under her arm Mrs. Bache carried a complete set of texts for
her science classes, although there were no classes until Monday.
She felt strangely vulnerable and bare when she carried no books.
To chapels, to meals, to student affairs, to faculty meetings, she
brought her three weighty textbooks. The students who could
not comprehend her need of protection by her books were convinced that the books were full of marginalia and underlinings,
valuable clues to future quizzes. In reality there were no marks
in the books at all, only jottings of thoughts and quotations from
poems on the end-pages, made at moments in staff meetings
(she and her laboratory assistant, a graduate student from a
nearby college who helped out three days a week, constituted
the "Science Staff") during which her assistant explained complex physical experiments which she could not follow. She would
assume an air of intense concentration as she took notes, to
avoid the impossible effort to understand. At the back of *Modern Biology* she had written:

Israel Human Rights Day, 1958 stamp. Slab of stone in-
scribed with Hebrew reading "Thou Shalt Love Thy Neighbor
as Thyself."

E. Rankin says she contributed to an Arab Relief Fund. Probably also packed up used clothing for needy Nazis twenty years
ago.

Similarity between trial of Adolph Eichmann and Henry
Wirtz. Wirtz too pleaded carrying out orders from above, he
too was intelligent and perverted. Human beings have made
very little progress.

Send to Jack Rubin for new stamp issued on 29th anniversary of death of Rabbi Ba'al Shem Tov. Issued August 21. Who was he?

The end-pages of *Using Chemistry: Problems* contained a few formulas, crossed out and reworked, and the notes:

Show Ellen, from MacLeish's piece on Hemingway's death: "But it is not enough to see and touch and know: one must have memories of love and pain and death." Fits with theory of hers that even now W. Wordsworth's thing about art as recollection in tranquillity is held. Experience alone not enough. It must all lie first in a bed of memory before one can write.

Rabbi Ba'al Shem Tov: b. 1700–d. 1760. Chassidist. Believed humility necessary to those in high places on the earth. The sad and the lonely ones must strive for joy. In worship a state approaching ecstasy is needed. I think: how modern worship is so far from this, so automatic and cold. We hear lectures on books, a little Talmud is read, we wish each other good *shabbos* and go home until the next week. The remnants . . . perhaps there is something to the maintaining of strict ritual. Perhaps it is the media (medium? which?) to reach this 'ecstasy.'

Her textbooks clutched under her arm, Ernestine Bache, widow, philatelist, ex-citizen of Buchenwald, passionate Zionist, perpetual exile, grown suspicious in her Jewishness of the whole Gentile world, and teacher of science because she is afraid to trust herself in the emotional baths and personal revelations of beloved literature or music, went to breakfast.

CHAPTER II

The Buttery

Ellen Acton found Meg Miers drawing coffee from the standing urn. Millicent, the pale-faced town girl who "came in" to work in the kitchen, handed her a cup and saucer.

"How's the coffee?"

Meg shook her head. "I don't know yet. The color is about the same as usual. But I haven't bitten in yet. This morning I'm prepared. I've already eaten so it won't kill my appetite."

Meg taught art. Her method was simplicity itself. Each morning she set out all the materials for the creation of pictures, sculptures and allied arts on the long shiny drawing tables of the Art Room, arranged books of sketches, apples, pieces of voile, and miniature busts of Caesar and Beethoven at the ends of the tables. She then retired to an easel set up at one end of the room on a prominence from which she could watch the class, and went on with her own work. A student energetic enough to traverse the distance to Miss Miers's platform could learn a great deal by watching her paint her delicate and charming landscapes. Her technique and knowledge improved in the long mornings and afternoons, during chapels which she rarely attended and classes which scrupulously she did, was developing rapidly. She was slowly coming closer to finding her own style, and she was grateful to her students' innate lethargy which precluded too many interruptions in her development. Meg's single-minded devotion to her canvases was extended to a talent for friendship. Ellen came often to the Art Room, ate the remains of bowls of fruit and loaves of French bread that had been misrepresented in students' still lifes on the walls, and was grateful for Meg's bemused, monosyllabic response to her troubles. Painting constantly as she listened, she managed to provide Ellen's troubled spirit with the safety of distance.

Ellen sat down at her assigned place at the head of Table Three, Meg across the aisle at Six. Students straggled in, scraping their chairs as they pulled them out, drooping at once into attitudes of early-morning dejection. Dressed in clothes that seemed to be rescued from parts of other costumes, or in jeans and sweaters to which the knees and elbows were bloated appendages, the students on Saturday were a shipwrecked remnant of their weekday, uniformed elegance. Slowly the nine long tables filled. Cocoa jugs steamed in the center of the tables, and piles of buttered buns stirred fitfully each time a new arrival's foot hit a table leg.

Across the room Miss Rankin sat at the head of Nine, making pencil marks on a pad of legal-sized yellow paper. Beside her place and taped to the oilcloth lay the seating chart, the precise shape of the Buttery itself. Millicent regularly placed Miss Rankin's fork and coffee cup over this chart, and the Assistant Headmistress, with a gesture that suggested her profound annoyance with all human imperfection, would clear the chart the moment she sat down. Looking quickly from the chart to the empty places at the tables to the yellow pad, she took attendance, her presence, by a special quality of rectitude that emanated from her, a reproof to the late-comers and the absent, although she said nothing. To the uncombed young at her table, her tightly drawn-back gray hair, still reminiscently red in the bun, was a silent example of neatness. Miss Rankin always said she liked "to handle freshmen" when assignments for counselling were being discussed; and the rest of the faculty suspected it was because she feared the initial, fatal, debilitating effect of another adviser's softness.

The Buttery was now almost full. The Headmistress, temporarily deflected from breakfast (a meal to which she was devoted and at which she ate hugely) by a tangential errand of picking up the candy wrappers that had collected among the ivy beneath the study hall window and which she had spotted as she made her way across the campus, was absent from her place at Senior One table. The carillon struck nine, paused, and then launched again into the morning hymn. Trudy Langer, red-faced from finding no letter from Jamie in her box (although he had never written to her and she had no reason to expect one), flopped into her seat at Senior One. Ruthie Vandermeer, right behind her, almost fell over her as she stumbled into the seat beside her. Miss Rankin noted their late arrival with a mark on the yellow pad, a feat she accomplished without being seen to look up.

Millicent poised in the doorway from the kitchen, smiling her foolish smile.

"More buns?"

"We're fine, thanks, Millie," said Meg. Milly bobbed up and down, as she had seen done at the movies, and went back into the kitchen. Jo Long and Robbie Parks in their places at the Junior tables were eating stolidly. Each of them without looking as the other quartered her bun, buttered it, and inspected the piece before she ate it. They ate with the precision and rapport of members of a well-trained water ballet.

Lucy Moore strode in toward her table, her white Savage School blazer immaculate. She was out of breath and shining with perspiration.

"Morning, dearie," she said breathlessly to Ellen as she passed. Ellen, gulping the hot, tasteless coffee ("sometimes I offer it up as penance," she once told Meg), looked up at Lucy and smiled.

"What do you do the mile in?"

"It's according to where the mile is. At Williams I make

very good time, especially if John Fish is pacing me." Lucy was engaged to John Fish. It was impossible for her to keep his name out of her conversation.

The Headmistress rushed in and stood at her place. At her table the girls straggled to their feet without looking at her, a caricature of respect. With one hand she gestured to the girls to be seated and with the other tried desperately to restore the strings of her hair to their places. She sat down, saying:

"ForthisfoodwhichweareabouttoreceiveLordwethankThee."

Unobtrusively Ellen crossed herself. The only Catholic on the faculty, she was often caught between the observances, almost involuntary, of her lifetime and her role as a well-assimilated and therefore acceptable representative of the Faith in the staunch Protestant citadel of Miss Hands. Usually she compromised, made a small cross low on her diaphragm just below the level of the table, looking at her plate as she did so.

Madame Mifflin and Mrs. Bache, allied for the moment in their joint lateness, slipped quietly into their places. The Headmistress, ignoring her own late arrival, frowned at them. They sat down at the sophomore tables, which immediately fell silent.

Trudy Langer crammed her third buttered bun into her mouth, swallowed the cocoa in one gulp so that her mouth ached as she put the cup down, and said:

"May I be excused please, Miss Blount?"

The Headmistress seemed to wrestle with the rules as she knew them. Trudy stared at her, her high, barren forehead and lank yellow hair appealing to Miss Blount for permission to escape. Glancing briefly at Miss Rankin, who had made the rule that no student could be excused until the meal was over, she said in a low voice:

"Of course, dear."

Trudy rushed for the door.

"And . . . Trudy . . ."

She stopped, and half-turned.

"You won't be late for Chapel?"

Trudy said no.

Her departure stimulated every student into action. Mumbling excuses to the teacher at the end of their table, one after the other shuffled out of the Buttery, their sneakers making sucking noises against the linoleum floor. Miss Rankin wrote a note on the top of a yellow sheet. The rule about leaving the Buttery after meals was now destined for more impressive reiteration, in print, in next year's Student Handbook.

Outside on the steps, Ruthie Vandermeer, Nan Kittredge and Trudy Langer lounged against an ancient pillar whose fluting was disrupted by peeling paint. Absent-mindedly Trudy stripped and curled pieces of paint around her finger.

"God, I wish I had a cigarette."

"We could have one if we had the key to the stage. Seward has it. Let's ask her." Ruthie's deep ambition to be loved always involved doing whatever anyone suggested. For some time now, ever since the new Arts Hall had been built, backstage had been their hideout where they went to sit and, in cabalistic fashion, to smoke. It was possible to enter it through the auditorium, but with the key they were relatively safe: they could lock themselves and their great clouds of smoke into the small aperture.

"Ask her, my foot. She'll know why we want it."

"Maybe Acton has one too. She was backstage last night." Nan Kittredge, who was short, fat and amiable, was a born conformist, and whenever possible covered her tendencies with an outward show of revolt.

Trudy was not to be comforted by this gratification of her wishes. She respected Miss Acton but to admit it she felt would reduce her status before the others. Her reputation for rebellion was too valuable to her.

"Actually, I'm thinking of drumming Acton out of the Scurvy Elephant Society. I thought last night she disliked what we were doing to Seward."

Nan looked surprised. "How, disliked?"

"Oh, you could tell she thought all the horsing around was mean, and a couple of times she told Emily Courtney to shut up. Oh, I suppose she's still a Scurvy Elephant at heart but she's getting old. Giving in to the Little Fox Rankin is easier."

The Scurvy Elephant Society was a spontaneous growth, of recent incorporation. Nan Kittredge's mother, who sent her long, amusing letters full of domestic anecdotes, had written that Tommie came home from second grade and said his teacher had called him a scurvy elephant. Indignant investigation had revealed that he had been called a "disturbing element." Trudy, whose ear for such things was quick, had founded the Society on the spot, and to it she invited all the senior class's more dissident elements. The Society prided itself on meeting without appointment and on admitting to membership only tried and true rebels who had acted as well as talked. This was the theory; actually, in the months of its existence, it had established itself nowhere so concretely as in the talk of its members. Cigarettes smoked surreptitiously, trips into town without signing out (and getting back in without being challenged) were the major revolutionary acts of the Scurvy Elephants.

The Society at an early meeting had drawn up (but never written down, for fear of detection, and pure laziness) a constitution, one item of which stated that "in order to form a more perfect union of dissident creatures it is resolved that before graduation the society will be effective in ridding the student body of that gibbering goon, Miss Seward." The adjectives had been selected by Trudy, who also nominated Miss Acton and Miss Miers to be members emeriti. But to date no one had summoned up the courage to inform the faculty members of their election.

Nan's membership stemmed from her contribution of the inspired name. Now she felt compelled by her innate conformism to suggest some positive action against authority.

"I'll go look for the key in Seward's room if you want, Trudy. They're all still stuffing their faces in the Buttery, and she's such a queery she'll think she's lost it."

"Hell no," said Trudy, feeling her leadership slipping. "I'll get it. I'll meet you in Arts in ten minutes. We've still time before that ghastly Chapel. Pick up your feet, girls . . ."

Trudy rolled her jeans to her knees and went off at a trot, her ponytail swinging behind her. The others strolled along the edges of the path, being careful to walk only on the grass, Miss Rankin having just recently issued strict injunctions against it. They came up to Emily Courtney and Joy Jennings, both members in good standing, and continued with them toward Arts. The Scurvy Elephant Society was gathering for its after-breakfast cell meeting.

The faculty lingered in the Buttery, atomized, separated from each other by long, messy tables. Millicent made her way slowly among them. She smiled at the napkins and soiled silver, and made a special trip to the kitchen for each crumpled napkin. Her idiocy always irritated Miss Rankin who had tried without any success to get her to consolidate her efforts, stack dishes and use a tray. Millicent smiled at her, showing flat layers of gold and silver between her teeth, nodded yes, uncomprehendingly, and went back to making a trip to the kitchen with each item.

Meg Miers looked about. "Why don't we consolidate?"

Miss Rankin, still making notes, had discerned a small coffee spot on the cuff of her white blouse. Irritably she dabbed at it with a napkin she had dampened in her water glass, and stayed seated where she was. In an unconscious acknowledgment of authority the rest of the faculty moved to the Headmistress's table. The Headmistress smiled, feeling pleased. To show her democracy she decided to gossip:

"Did you all see the announcement about Pamela Ames?"

"No," said Ellen, "did she finally graduate from Lasell? They must have got the simple declarative sentence across to her somehow."

"I think she went to Bennett Junior," said the Headmistress, suddenly feeling unsure of her ground and not wishing to have the conversation move out of the successfully launched ex-student groove.

"You must mean *Eleanor* Ames." Miss Rankin's voice was hard and sour. Members of the same family who had been students at Miss Hands could never be certain of being assigned their proper first names by the Headmistress. Miss Rankin used the same irritated tone in correcting the Headmistress that she relied upon to reduce to confusion a student who gave a stupid answer in analytical geometry. The Headmistress's inability to separate in her mind members of a family she took to be another example of her unfitness to rule and made certain everyone noticed it.

To create a diversion and because she could not bear to watch the Headmistress being victimized, Meg spoke in her soft drawl which made everything she said oddly pleasant:

"I see by this morning's *Times* that the Headmaster of St. James School got fired for punishing a lad by stuffing him into the clothes dryer."

"What was the crime?" asked Ellen.

"How terrible," said Miss Blount.

"It said the boy forgot to wear his rubbers," said Meg, enjoying herself. By her own special means of indirect reference, she too was capable of cruelty to the Headmistress.

"*Terrible*," said the Headmistress again.

"Is that all?" asked Jo.

"What do you mean, is that all?"

"I mean, no positive action?"

"Yes," said Meg, deliberately misunderstanding, "I think he then turned on the gas for a few seconds."

"Oh good," said Jo. "That sounds like fine educational procedure."

Mrs. Bache was offended by the tone of the talk. "It was not so funny in Europe."

The door pushed open. Sophie Seward, dishevelled and wet at

the temples, came in. She put her trench coat over a chair, held a cup under the spout of the urn and, disturbed by the numbers at the Headmistress's table, sat down with Miss Rankin. Miss Rankin went on writing.

Sophie's cup was only half filled with black lees. Her shaking hands tried to clear a place for it amid the littered remains of a student's breakfast. Miss Rankin looked annoyed at the sound of the napkin moving fruitlessly over the oilcloth.

"Millicent," shrilled Miss Rankin's high voice, "come and clear this place."

Sophie abandoned her efforts at once. Millicent shuffled in, smiling her bland and empty smile. She picked up a piece of bun wrapped in a napkin and started for the kitchen.

"More at once," roared Miss Rankin, close to losing control, but Millicent was almost back to the kitchen and nothing could interrupt her determined progress.

"I'm sorry to be late. My alarm clock . . ." Her voice, full of nerves and self-doubts, trailed off. "It's begun to rain . . ."

"Just what was he fined for?" asked Robbie who was enjoying the story because she could see Jo was.

"I can't recall exactly, but I think the judge said the chap was guilty of 'a serious error in judgment,'" said Meg. No longer interested herself, she was creating a sunset landscape out of coffee spots on the yellow oilcloth.

"A Turner—or maybe a Landseer," she said to Ellen, elaborating upon a hill with a red correcting pencil.

Almost to herself the Headmistress repeated her judgment upon the Headmaster of St. James. Miss Blount was proud of her inability to bear any form of physical violence, and this professed abhorrence kept her unaware that her own form of punishment, a subtle blend of useful gossip, almost-forgotten half-truths and persisting recriminations about a single, ancient blunder, was far more deadly to an erring student. Miss Blount spoke often to her faculty advisers of compassion but she herself never forgot a misstep and never failed to use it tellingly

against a student she had no special, economic reasons to defend.

Jo Long moved over to sit beside Sophie and recapped for
her in a low voice Meg's news item.

Robbie said in a loud voice: "There are all kinds of torture
and punishment. I read of a boy who died of fright when someone put a live mouse in his mouth."

Robbie's voice was projected toward Sophie and coated with
cruelty. Watching Jo across the room prodded a vagrant memory
of Sophie's terror of contact with small animals, the night in
her room when she thought a rat was in one of her drawers. . . .

Tears were in Sophie's eyes at once. She shuddered, but said
nothing.

Jo blinked angrily at Robbie and then said deliberately to
Sophie, making no attempt to lower her voice:

"What are your plans after Commencement?"

"I don't . . . really know . . . quite yet. I need a job to
carry me through the summer, and to pay back . . . debts. I'm
waiting to hear from one. A summer tutoring school."

"Would you like to stay with us for a week or so? On the
Cape?"

Sophie's head shook.

"How nice of you. I would love it. How . . . very nice of you.
I'll let you know as soon as I hear when the job starts."

Jo went back to Senior One. Looking from her paper to her
watch, Miss Rankin then stood up.

"A quarter to ten. Chapel is scheduled for ten."

Teaching for so many years, the faculty had long ago abdicated any real sense of time in deference to the mythical God
of the Schedule. The Daily Schedule, a variation upon the General Schedule, was posted each morning upon the school's four
bulletin boards. It contained deviations from the set time system, and represented the only hope of change for the day ahead
from the days past. Hung, strung, suspended, stretched upon
the sacred Schedule like Procrustes, the faculty found clocks unnecessary and lived instead by bells, guarded from the reality of

time by Miss Rankin's schedule. It was the *deus ex machina* of their lives. Obediently they filed out of the Buttery.

Meg erased her Turner with the sleeve of her smock and walked with Ellen.

"The mistress of novices keeps right at it. It'll be nice when we're professed," said Ellen.

Meg missed the allusion but caught the bitterness in her tone.

"Cheer up, kid, only one more week and we'll be sprung."

Ellen said: "Oh hell. I left my hymnal in my room again. *Mea culpa.* Have I time to go back for it?"

"Sure. And pick up my *Times* when you come. You can look at it during the standings-up and the sittings-down. You might as well have a good sin to confess this week."

"I never have any trouble filling the time. Not this year."

Ellen had learned to field all references to her religious practices in the same tone of amused tolerance with which they were tossed at her. She knew Meg regarded her Catholicism as charming, picturesque and anachronistic, but this no longer bothered her. Sometimes she wondered if this loss of edge, this failure to react to jokes and intellectual touches of scorn was not a sign that her faith, softening as it broadened, was weakening as well. Into the present air of jocular good humor between her and her friends on the faculty she resisted introducing a new hostile note, or objecting to the old ones. Meg of course was an exception. She professed a faith in Walter Pater ("*Pater noster* is the way all good prayers begin, isn't that true, Ellen?"), and joked with Ellen because her loving soul found all the practices of human beings merely useful facts to be added to her general knowledge of the pictorial world. And Madame made no reference at all to "that Faith" as she called it, pretending that her own new and militant Methodism could smother the parent faith by ignoring it, so that finally it would be buried in the eternal silence of reformation.

Sophie stayed behind. Millicent stood before her.

" 'Nother bun? Saved some in the kitchen. Have another?"

Sophie looked at her in silence. First Jo, then this innocent. Sophie nodded her head, unable to stand another kindness. Millicent shuffled away, her foolish smile wiped away by the sight of tears running down the face of the shaking teacher.

Captain Harrison Seward, U.S.N., had been responsible for what Sophie was, for Sophie and for Rickley, her younger brother by ten months. Captain Seward had been widowed at twenty-nine, his wife, a slight, uncommunicative, almost nonexistent woman, having, to his mind, been inconsiderate enough to die suddenly while he was on sea duty. He regarded his sister's call home as undignified. It involved being lowered from his ship to a ridiculously small outboard which took him through a choppy bay to port, an airplane flight to La Guardia Airport, and a taxi to Newark where his wife was to be buried in her family plot. From the moment he stepped into the outboard he was seasick, and he did not recover fully until the day after the funeral. For this, even more than for her inconsiderate choice of dying time, he never forgave her. He was a man whose life depended for its very continuance on routine. He could not bear innovations or disruptions of his plans; they ruined his temper and, he was now discovering, his stomach as well.

He arrived in Newark just in time to see the coffin being lowered into the ground. At the graveside stood his son and daughter, Sophie clinging to the smaller Rick, both staring uncomprehendingly from their mother in a box beneath the level of their feet, to their father in crumpled whites who had miraculously appeared, presumably on one of his rare and unexpected leaves. They saw no clear connection between the two events. Beside them were Captain Seward's two brothers-in-law, and his Great Aunt Sophia. A few stragglers lingered to watch, the minister read the last grim words, Aunt Sophia performed the ceremony of dropping dust onto the coffin, the Captain put on his gilded cap. It was all over. Sophie could remember that her sole con-

cern during the ceremony, in fact from the moment that blood
had gushed in a great bubble from her mother's mouth as she
stood weakly in the kitchen holding herself up on the stove,
had been for Rickley. As long as he did not cry everything was
all right with Sophie. What she could not bear was her fear that
his heart might break.

The Captain's general air of impatience stemmed the children's emotion at seeing him although, truth to tell, to them he
was more a complex symbol of King Arthur, Johnny Tremain
and Lord Horatio Nelson than a father of flesh. Only his irasci-
bility seemed real. Their sobs finally broke out during the
hushed and overwrought lunch served to them by their aunts
in a small, hot, duplex house on the outskirts of the city. "Belay that," he said sternly to them, and they did not cry in his
presence again. The Captain's concentrated stare, as if he were
searching the horizon for a missing segment of the fleet, was
interpreted by them to be disapproval; actually he had not yet
got his land legs and was worried about digesting the heavy
lunch in the intolerable heat.

After futile attempts to find a relative willing to harbor two
small, frightened, underweight children (he with acute acne, she
with asthma), Captain Seward registered them in schools two
states apart. They stood by as he slammed shut his suitcases
(they had waited in vain for the arrival of a sea chest, like the
Captain in James Barrie, but it seemed that he did not own
one), patted them on the head, told them to behave, and set
off to rejoin his task force, his step ebullient with his new sense
of freedom. He had always secretly believed that a good line
officer was better off unmarried. His marriage had been a weakness in his immaculate picture of himself. Now he felt as if he
had returned to his original chaste and dedicated concept.

The parting between the children was agonizing. Great Aunt
Sophia had them with her for two days before they left for
their schools. At the last Sophie locked her fingers with Rickley's and refused to let go. She did not cry, fearing that the
burden of Rickley's grief would be too great for her to bear.

The acne on Rickley's face stood out sharply, thrown into livid relief by his violent embarrassment. Sophie interpreted this as sorrow. Her breathing came in long-delayed, agonizing gasps, as if it were being pushed out of her lungs by a hesitant fist that opened and shut just too late. Finally she lost all control, and when Great Aunt Sophia unclasped their hands by digging her nails into Sophie's knuckles, and lifted Rickley aboard the train to Springfield, she shouted over and over, "I won't forget you, Rick. I won't forget you, Rick. I won't forget you . . ."

"Goodbye. I won't forget," called Rickley who felt acutely embarrassed at the scene his sister was making.

Sophie never did. In the week after her mother's death, she had found it easier to breathe at night if she pretended to be certain that her father intended to take her with him when he left for sea. Now, as each vacation approached, she daydreamed through her belief that Rickley would be at Aunt Sophia's; she pictured to herself their joyful reunion, the resumption of their old secrets and confessions. Her memory of him standing on the steps of the train, promising to remember her, was ineradicable, and the more she called it up, the more it became embellished with tears covering the red areas of Rickley's face, and the number of repetitions of his vows multiplied. Her own sorrow was now transferred to him; her agony, now that she had erased herself from her memory, belonged to him.

Rickley wrote to her in Northampton once. He spent his vacations visiting school friends or at camp in Maine to which he went directly after the spring semester ended. Sophie sat in Great Aunt Sophia's front room in Boston, sewing and reading aloud from *Middlemarch*, which she could not entirely understand although she felt a deep sympathy with Dorothea Brooke. She was waiting for someone to come back, although after a while she was not quite sure who—her mother, her father, her brother? She outgrew her asthma, but in her memory Rickley retained his acne, because she could not imagine herself loving him without it, his thin, bony, boyish arms, his high voice promising to remember her.

College made little change in Sophie's life. She still travelled from Boston to Northampton and back again for each vacation, she studied psychology with the vague aim of teaching, although her college was loftily addicted to the liberal arts and made no specific provisions for teaching certificates. She made few friends. She learned to smoke. It was during her first trial cigarette that she discovered the tremor in her fingers and hands. At times of stress it became acute, and her instructors complained that her examinations were almost unreadable.

In her junior year she was informed of her father's death at sea of a cerebral hemorrhage. The news brought her an immediate vision: she saw him standing on his bridge watching a mistaken scramble of ships under his command, out of line and out of order. She heard his great, raucous voice bellowing, over and over again in ever-greater volume, "belay that, belay that, BELAY THAT . . ." a great rush of blood from his vocal cords to his tightly capped forehead, and then death. He left nothing except his cases of uniforms, ribbons, a thick packet of papers and old orders, and two out dated but rarely worn civilian suits, for he had been a man who was never sure of himself and his significance when he was out of uniform.

Great Aunt Sophia stored his things that had been shipped to her in her hall closet. And then she did a strange thing: she satisfied her own need for importance by leaving her brother's naval hat, its gold decorations suitably tarnished by sea air, hanging permanently on the open peg in the front hall, to accompany a visitor's straw or bowler and her own furled umbrella.

In the wisdom of her majority, and with the aid of new insight provided by her psychology courses, Sophie was now able to realize that she had as much sense of her father, his cap hanging in the hallway and his body deep in the Pacific, as she had ever had of him in his lifetime. As she prepared tea in the butler's pantry for Great Aunt Sophia's Tuesday Club she could almost see him, on leave and dressed for breakfast in full uniform, issuing orders to the housemaid, to his sister, to Rickley, in naval jargon they could hardly understand and which he had always stubbornly refused to translate into what he called the speech of civilians. Captain Seward had never come home to Sophie, but in an obsessional sense he never left her.

Sophie had one strange illusion which nourished her in all the long silence of her early life: that she could act. Ellen Acton was, years later, to point out to Sophie at a Dramatics Club meeting that the more introverted an adolescent girl the more this particular illusion fastens itself upon her, for only in the ingrown recesses of herself and in her daydreams does the truth, for her, really abide. In her outward life Sophie could hardly bear to meet someone new, and her breathing coarsened in her throat every time an instructor looked her way in class, but her inner vision converted her thin, shaking hands to the nervous, significant gestures of a Tennessee Williams heroine, her asthmatic voice to the low, breathless tones of Medea and Portia and Major Barbara, and her sharp, almost fleshless features to the pert, rounded, sexual face of the motion-picture queen. All the tenuous neurasthenia which was genuine in Sophie was, in her dream, necessarily translated into the relaxed and magnetic charm of the actress.

At the beginning of her senior year in college, she decided to try out for a role in a play. She went to The Barn, where rehearsals were held, and allowed herself to be shepherded into a row of seats by a self-assured member of Actors. A black-haired girl with a ringing voice and heavy, constantly gesticulating hands described the parts. She then separated the candidates into groups according to the role they wished to audition for. Sophie thought perhaps the mother would suit her—already she had instinctively abdicated all thought of achieving the ingenue. She went over to a corner to sit with other candidates for Mother, and watched those before her intently as they read their way through sections of the part. Each candidate's eagerness to impress the dark-haired girl, who turned out to be the director, gave to her interpretation a feverish urgency, almost like characters in a suspense play talking against the approach of the moment of threatened disaster; finally this desperation overflowed the stage and reached Sophie in her seat. When her turn came she got up and left. Her flight thus made it possible for her to cherish her illusion a little longer without submitting it to a test. She believed, even in the face of her violently vibrating hands and her unpleasantly audible breathing as she left The Barn, that if she'd stayed she would have won the part, just as, obscurely, she still held fast to her belief that her father would have taken her with him, if only she'd been able to ask him in the right words, that Rickley might have written to her again if her answer to his one letter had not been so weak and inept, so self-pitying.

Three months before her graduation, at a poetry reading by a famed but reluctant New England poet, Sophie met Lucius Clements. He was an assistant in the English department, a weak-looking, light-haired, stringy young man whose ears lay tight against his head, almost as if they had been sketched onto the oval of his head, and whose eyes had the reddened, ineffectual look of an albino. He and Sophie walked the hilly streets of Northampton, drank wine with their dinners at Wiggins Tavern, and talked about George Meredith, on whom he was planning to write his Ph.D. thesis. Blinking in the candlelight of the tavern, Lucius watched Sophie's shaking fingers fumble for a cigarette, and talked. Night after night, in carefully parcelled installments, Lucius, who in the heat of his confidences had asked Sophie to call him Luke, unburdened himself to her. She listened and nodded regularly, agreeably, the bob of her head punctuating his narrative. Of all the great, flowing mass, she later remembered only parts:

"My mother believed in me, perhaps too much. My father hated me because of that. Neither of us cared much for him."

"I stole a great many things, from my father, from stores, especially bookstores, and from the boys at school, mostly money. I was never caught or even suspected. If I hadn't always done so well at school and at college I might have done very well at thievery."

"I have never believed in God. I've never needed to. I can

think of only two reasons for doing so: if I decided to make the priesthood my profession, and if stigmata suddenly appeared on my hands and feet—on Good Friday."

"I've never known a woman of intellect, which leads me to believe that she does not exist except in fiction, and in the highly romantic memoirs of the friends of Margaret Fuller, George Eliot, George Sand and Madame de Récamier."

Sophie, whose memories of George Eliot were now indistinct and tied unpleasantly to the parlor in Aunt Sophia's house, said little. Indeed it would have been hard to contribute very much to Luke's conversations. He used the first-person-singular pronoun in a regular, rhythmical way so that Sophie was lulled into silence by its hypnotic recurrence.

Luke was interested in Sophie only as an ear, until one night. They were having dinner in his rooms. During the chicken cacciatore, which he had prepared himself with a rather heavy dosing of herbs and many gestures, his red-rimmed eyes filled suddenly with tears.

"Oh Sophie, let me try to sleep with you."

Sophie wondered afterwards why she had not heard the note of despair in the diction of his sentence. She was moved by a desperate sense of being needed, but this was an egoistical sentiment. She was entirely unaware of Luke's sudden and pathetic loss of aggressive egoism.

Their trial was an excoriating failure. Once in bed, panic and moral fears, and the reading of too much graphic modern fiction, froze Sophie into inept withdrawal. Luke's sudden flare of violence disintegrated at once before Sophie's clenched rigidity. Luke was pathetic, almost speechless in his incapability. Afterwards they could not look at each other. They dressed in an atmosphere of distaste that battlefield commanders must feel for each other as they meet in a tent after a decisive defeat. Their next meeting was like the reunion of fatally ill members of a family who know the truth about each other, but not about themselves. They recognized failure in each other and knew where to place the blame, and they each had had time to bury in unconsciousness their memory of their own role in the fiasco. Luke was well experienced in this kind of deception; he was no novice to sexual failure.

After that evening he never called again. In Sophie's mind his face became merged with Rickley's and her father's. Sometimes she saw it adorned with a military cap, flecked with patches of acne. At the end of the semester she heard he'd gone to teach in a boy's preparatory school in the South. She never saw him again.

During the War, while she was teaching English in a school outside of Boston (her liberal arts degree was acceptable only in private schools where the need for teachers who would work for substandard salaries was greater than their concern for certificates, and they were mercifully free of state regulations), she embarked on another of her failure-destined missions, on what she had come by now to think of as a career in loss. Her marriage of three months ended when her husband, a young, frightened medical corpsman, died at Guadalcanal. She had met him at a party given by the school for servicemen at a nearby base. Five years younger than she, there had been something in his cornered look, his eyes full of the appeal of a man retreating from a rout, that touched her. Their marriage was an arrangement of a few weeks, a legal arrangement she entered into because he would have her on no other terms.

They married in June. This time Sophie shut her eyes and prayed to be adequate to her husband's haste and anxiety, and in a fumbling, accidental way, she was. In August he was dead. When she returned to her school in September she wore no wedding ring, and had already abandoned his name, which was Larkin. All that remained with her of the soldier was his insignia which she put away in the bottom of her jewel case, the marriage license, and the child she carried, quite unobserved, until Christmas recess. Before he died he had time to write her one letter, in the small, agonizingly cramped handwriting that was partly a symbol of a disturbed mind and partly the exigencies of writing on miniature V-mail forms. She recognized the letter to be one torn from the very depths of his personal anguish, and she mourned as much for this grief in which she played no part as for him:

Dear Sophie:

I am well except for this thing that happened to me. I haven't slept too much since it happened but I'll write about it to you so when you see me again you'll know if I seem different. Well, we were sent down this gully to pick up a Marine who'd been hurt very bad. It was our first job after we got on, and the Marine'd been down there for some time now due to a sniper that was covering the road down and doing a good job of it.

Well we got down there and hoisted him onto a litter. He was a heavy guy and the legs of his pants were caked solid with blood. We moved carefully along the ledge. After a while it got wider and then we saw a light patch that seemed like a short cut back to the upper side of the gulley. Joe Lynch, he's the guy that was sent down with me, says let's go that way because this Marine was damned heavy and getting heavier all the time. His arms had fallen over the edge of the litter and that made it even harder. The less we had to walk the better and the road on each side of the patch was deep mud.

Well we went that way, and as soon as we got into it and felt it I knew damned well what it was. The sand pulled at my boots until my heels felt like they were tearing off. Joe shouted at me at the same time I was shouting at him. We were both going down, slow but sure. Joe put down his end of the litter and grabbed a branch above his head. I was left with the litter end up on my side and I couldn't move without Joe. And all the time there's this sand, like fists, pulling at my feet. I couldn't see my boots any more. Well then, I put my end down and grabbed at a tree root sticking out of the mud. I thought, God knows this is true, that it would be easier to move that litter out, from the side of the sand pit, if I got free first, than from right in it. I thought I'd pull my arms out from their sockets before I got loose. When I swung back over to the bank Joe Lynch was standing there crossing himself and yanking at a medal on his neck big as a silver dollar. "Jesus Mary and Joseph," he kept saying.

Well then we started back. And God Sophie, do you know, there was nothing there. Nothing—no litter, no shot-up Marine, nothing. In that little time while we got out, that whole thing had sunk into the pit. The Marine must have passed out before we even got to the sand pit, because he never made a sound, just lay there and sank away.

Every time I lay down I think about that branch I pulled on. If I hadn't seen it I wouldn't have put down that boy. If he hadn't been out cold he would have yelled when he knew he was going in. All ifs, but I can't sleep trying to think about how it could have been different.

Well, what's the use? I just thought I'd write. I'm well and hope this finds you the same. It'll be a while yet, I guess. Sometimes now I'm glad. Maybe I can do something right before this is over and I come home. Love, Louis.

Louis's son, whom she had named John in her planning, was born on Christmas Day. Sophie never saw him. The poor, semi-human creature, his legs one long, undifferentiated mass, lived one hour and mercifully died. Sophie absorbed the news as she had every other desertion. By now it seemed inevitable that she would move through life being warmed briefly by the touch of another human being and then thrust back into the darkness of a personal outer space.

In the next six years Sophie taught in five secondary schools, all of them for girls, all of them private. A brief flare of confidence in her, as she presented her credentials and wrote her sensitive, beautifully composed letters of application, a little period of tentative faculty friendliness in the first few months after arrival, and then the inevitable rejection would begin. The students, who withheld judgment long enough to decide who would dominate the battlefield of the classroom, found her high, whispering voice, all that remained of the years of desperate, asthmatic breathing, very funny, and her shaking hands that constantly lost the place in the text, dropped pencils and wrote a spastic script on the board, worthy objects of satire. They found it easy to make her jump at a slight noise and some classes, particularly those she devoted entirely to grammar or *Silas Marner*, were often a steady tattoo of objects gravitating abruptly to the floor.

The cruelest moments came when Sophie tried to teach them Shakespeare. Caught and held fast by the stirring beauty of the words, she would forget herself as she read aloud. Unaware of the dichotomy between the little, almost voiceless, shaking woman she was, and the grandeur of the pleading Desdemona, the deeply offended Gertrude, the lost and crazed Lady Macbeth, she would often get deep into a scene, feeling her love of it to be creating an absolute and inviolable dramatic moment, and would only slowly be made aware of a student aping her in the back row, or another grinning openly at a friend across the room.

The faculty retrieved their initial gift of confidence and never forgave her for becoming an object of ridicule to the students, a position which they instinctively felt weakened their own rather shaky ramparts in the pitched battle that was the normal faculty-student relationship.

Sophie's history now became a series of strategic retreats from her weaknesses. Emboldened at first by the fact of her marriage, she believed she could live alone, and so she applied for jobs at day schools. Her choice of flats was always dictated by her dramatic sense. She liked converted Victorian houses or renovated Revolutionary cantonments. Her eating habits were erratic and expensive so that by the middle of the month she was often without funds and forced to charge at the corner grocer whose end-of-month tally, unitemized, reflected his keen intuition about Sophie's inability to challenge it, and her sinking financial situation. Sometimes she would make a desperate protest in which the tones of retreat were already audible:

"But Mr. Amadeo, can it really be that much? Only one person . . . I eat so little. . . ."

Mr. Amadeo, or Mr. Gustafson, or Mr. Rooney would always shrug:

"You want to sue me, Miss? It is what it is."

Two other traumatic events drove Sophie finally to accept the promised security of Miss Hands Faculty House. While she was teaching at the Millbrook School near San Francisco she had roomed on the second floor of a grim, narrow, Gold-Rush-days house. The four floors were connected by brown-stained stairs which curled abruptly, and the house's two bathrooms stood, one above the other, near the stairs on the second and third floors. Sophie rarely saw the other roomers, because she took her main meal at noon at the school and ate the others at a cafeteria. But in April she became aware of a noise in the room above her, a step-thump, step-thump. Going back and forth, over and back, as she prepared her classes for the next day, the enigmatic noise began to obsess her. She found herself lying on her bed fully dressed until the early hours of the morning, construing Kafka-like fantasies of roaches who lived and scrambled about thumping on the floor above her. She was like an escaped convict, straining for the sound of pursuing police; some nights she slept all night in her trench coat to be ready, she thought, her hand wrapped around the broom handle she used for propping up her window on hot nights.

One late afternoon, as she came in cold from her twenty-block walk from school, she met her landlady and had to listen to her grumble about the highway robbery committed by plumbers these days. The third-floor bathroom had been flooded by a defective toilet, and she'd waited all day for the "damned fool *union* plumber" to come. Sophie commiserated and went up to her room. Immediately the step-thump step-thump began. She lay down on her bed and stared, horrified, at the spotted ceiling. Then it stopped. She fell asleep, exhausted by her day, the race up the stairs to get away from the landlady, the terror that awaited her when she got there.

She woke to a dark room and could not tell what time it was. Back and forth across the room above her the noise went, and then, to her terror, it moved to the stair well. It increased in intensity and then, starting down the stairs, it seemed to rise to a horrifying crescendo of growing nearness. It was coming down! The walls of her room, the drums of her ears, the fibers and membranes of her mind were penetrated and flooded by it. Almost mad with fear, Sophie leaped for the door, fumbled shakingly for her latch and flung open the door. On the next to the last step stood a girl of twenty, her blonde hair hanging down her back. She wore a black silk shirt which clung to her breasts, an elegant pair of silk shorts. One leg, protruding from the short-shorts, was browned and beautifully tapered. The other was a light wood stump carved to a fine point at the end. It terminated in a boat-shaped piece which provided it with a base almost as broad as its capital, and it wore the same gilt-embroidered black ballet shoe as the other foot. Under the silk of her shorts the polished wood looked like the leg of a fine harpsichord covered with a decorative throw.

Sophie stepped back and slammed her door shut. The step-thump of the blonde girl passed her door, and went down the hall and into the bathroom. She could hear water running into the tub. *The landlady's diatribe against plumbers . . . she has to use the bathroom I use. She's climbing with her stump into the bathtub I take a bath in.* Sophie believed she could never wash in that room again, use that toilet again, come into close contact with that vile amputation, and she did so only with repugnance.

The final decision to live at her next school (next September it was to be Miss Hands) she made the day the Bible salesman came. He knocked on her door with a heavy Douay Bible under his arm, a book large enough to cover the whole top of Sophie's portable phonograph when he put it down. For six days she had spoken to no one. Afflicted with a streptococcus throat she had not gone to school, had had some food sent in from the delicatessen and had sat in her room, rereading stacks of letters, some dating back twenty-five years to the one from Rick-ley. She asked the Bible salesman to come in because she pitied his hot, red face and the apparent heaviness of his gold-clasped package, and because of her own desperate need to talk to some-one. After three hours, during which they sat on the edge of her bed in her dark, narrow little room and drank water alter-nately from her toothbrush glass and told each other the truths of their separate, accumulated lonelinesses, Sophie, a confirmed Unitarian, bought, on time, a thirty-seven dollar Catholic Bible. She knew she had to pay for his time, although at the end he had not pressed the sale. This involved her in seven-dollar-a-month payments during a period when her money had been coming to an end about the twelfth of the month. Now she would run out two days earlier. After the salesman had gone she knew for certain that she had arrived at the very shores of dark-ness, and that to live alone was for her a dangerous risk. No longer was she able to contain her desperation, to choose among human beings. Anyone, like the cornered listeners of the Ancient Mariner, was important to her if he would listen to her, and now she knew she would pay any price for it.

So began Sophie's year at Miss Hands. Her room was on the top floor (at her request, so that she would not hear the thump-ing of anyone above her, and it was an easy request to grant for there was no competition for a room three flights up). She filled her bookcase with yellow-backed plays from Samuel French, and she spent her evenings reading roles she thought might be suitable for her, if next summer she gathered the courage to . . . Her dresser had nothing on it but the oversized Bible which she had opened just once, to enter on its blank front page the names and vital dates of Captain Harrison Seward, U.S.N., Sophia Lucretia Seward, 1864–1947, Rickley Allen Seward, b. 1918, after which she wrote in her shaky script, "whereabouts unknown." Then she shut the Bible, latching the clasp. Perhaps because of a faulty mechanism in the lock, perhaps because of the shaking uncertainly of her fingers, she was never again able to get it open.

Ellen's notebook, May— 196—:

Of Ronald Firbank's books someone has said, E. Wilson, was it?: "a world so complete in itself you feel sure it must somewhere exist." So I feel about the world of Miss Hands. If I were to put it down in a book a critical remark something like this might be made, without any awareness on the part of the critic that it *does* exist, here.

Accidentally overheard two girls in the hall talking about the "Scurvy Elephant" Society that smokes cigarettes under the stage in the Arts Hall. Lovely name, but being of the enemy I'll probably never hear anything more about them until Rankin noses them out and the fur flies. I can make a guess about the membership, however.

Madame, the true *franc-tireur*. Today at lunch, after the girls had gone to field hockey—Lucy Moore bounding out after them like a delighted antelope—she sniped at us all, I for profaning Rousseau, Jo for making light of the French Revolution, Robbie for suggesting Juvenal's wit was superior to Voltaire's. We were all Peter Rabbits in Mr. MacGregor's brackish garden and she was shrilly furious. (May Sarton tells in her new book about a French teacher she once had, and says that as a result of her contact with her "it is hard for me even now to detach myself from the conviction I held at twelve years old that the French are superior in every way to everyone else.") For the moment Sophie was out of it, but no. Madame went on to describe the tumor she had had taken from her breast. Sophie looked white and shocked and shriveled. I think Seward's like a medical student who leaves every lecture hall suddenly stricken by whatever obscure disease has just been graphically described. I tried to head off Madame before she got well launched into the saga of the mother of Mary Tracy '60 who had a massive something or other. We had to hear just where the cut went, up the arm and down. Sophie left, hitting her knuckles against the door jamb in her rush to get out. Madame, hardly noticing and then grinning at the door as if to point up poor Sophie's oddity, advanced into brain tumors and open-heart operations she had heard and read about.

I think if the Head says again, "Everyone stand in their place" I shall resign in full sight of the whole chapel and join an Order. And yet, what an absurd reaction to a simple error! I wonder if women in convents rasp upon each other's nerves as we do here. Is this the universal condition of an unilateral society, that the sexual half lacking to us is filled out by all the excess viciousness left over from the half that remains? "Get thee to a nunnery," Hamlet says to Ophelia when the whole aspect of treacherous womanhood dismays him. I would say the same, in the same spirit, to Miss Hands' Ellen Acton.

CHAPTER III

Chapel

I N her room in Faculty House Miss Rankin was hastily changing her blouse. Her room, bare and angular and monastically lacking decoration, was arranged for efficiency. In dead center of the bureau stood a brown, square box. Within it, arranged by size and color, were rows of earrings, the only decoration she ever wore, and a collection of large pins which held her gray bun in its tight place. Her blouse off, she stood for a moment doing nothing, in an unaccustomed, luxurious spasm of inertia. She felt for her bun and the few stray strands that had escaped from it. Then, with the same swift motion that an infantryman uses just before he launches a hand grenade, she pulled the two crossed pins from her bun. Her hair fell to her waist, some of it still surprisingly red and vibrant. In its cascading eloquence the gray which had comprised the bun disappeared under the more insistent color. There was no mirror in her room. She had learned long ago to do her hair without its aid, and now she moved her fingers gently over the roots, enjoying for a moment a sense of freedom and release.

Elizabeth Rankin's pride had always been her hair. In a family of brunettes her light, lovely red curls had been the delight of her mother. While the small girl sat on a padded stool in her bedroom, Lena Rankin, sitting close beside her, would stroke the silky hair with a brush until it stood out in soft peaks around the tiny face, dwarfing it with its radiance. An only child, Elizabeth, whom her father called Liza, while her mother clung to the saint's name she had given her, early developed that curious aura of calm, removed self-possession that children so placed in a family often have. She seemed to exist on a plane a little higher than theirs; she moved effortlessly in the higher reaches of the well-contained world that the three of them had constructed, at first, for themselves, like the main organism, the vital principle, within a cocoon.

Sterling Rankin was small and dark, a man built on the lines of a boy. He looked, dressed for church which he attended regularly, like a fourteen-year-old about to present himself for Confirmation, in his narrow, blue-serge suit, his double cowlick, his ruddy boy's face. At thirteen Liza was exactly as tall as he, and because it was more comfortable for her and less conspicuous, she began to go to church with her father. They sat together solemnly, always in the same pew of the Protestant Episcopal Church in Des Moines, his dark head on a level with her flagrantly red one. They looked like a brother and sister sent to represent their parents who had chosen this Sunday to "sleep in." Lena Rankin was a Polish Catholic from Dubuque, Iowa, a woman of pallid coloring, slight build and no education: her name before her marriage had been Konski. Born and raised (until her father and five brothers in an unusual burst of familial energy moved the family, a great chest of linens and the proceeds of the sale of their farm) on a sprawling, prosperous farm outside of Lvov, she was hesitant about using English for anything but the simplest responses. After a few stumbling attempts to translate her inner thoughts from fluent mental Polish into scant vocal English, she surrendered to inhibition and a habitual, apologetic silence. Her family, strongly devoted to each other, never noticed her silences. They worked apart, kept long, hard hours, and were themselves untalkative people contentedly separated from each other all day. Their spacious, two-hundred-acre farm was almost an exact replica of the one they had left behind in the old country.

Her thin, sober, self-contained brothers and her father always called their livestock with feminine Polish names, and the talk that flowed occasionally between them after dinner, to which Lena listened with pleasure, was always in the abrupt, consonantal sounds of their native tongue. They knew very little of the new country, and they regarded the young feed-and-grain salesman's evident interest in Lena with wordless surprise.

Lena, swathed in garish white satin ordered from a mail-order house and too heavy for her frail shoulders and flat chest, stumbled as she passed the portals of the church on her wedding day. In her surprise that anyone, and especially a handsome, ebullient American, would wish to marry so unsuitable a girl, Lena did everything she could think of to close the gap between her forced silences and her husband's easy sentences. She enrolled in a night-school class during the first year of their marriage, but the progress of the other immigrants was too quick, and after the first few sessions, the instructor, impatient with her blank inability to answer, ignored her. She stayed home after midsemester and tried a self-help textbook. The first chapters went well. They contained words she already knew, but once embarked on English grammar she was completely lost, and Sterling's amusement when she could not comprehend transitive verbs discouraged her from further attempts.

At church suppers given by the Ladies Aid of Sterling's church she discovered that her homemade clothes were outlandish and her heavy English unequal to the small talk of her sex. On their first Christmas Eve together Sterling took her to a Grain Dealers' party at the Hotel Fort Des Moines. She was bewildered and pained by the evening. The talk swirled about her head and filled her ears with incomprehensible sounds; she was frightened into smiling continuously and, to the eyes of the other wives, foolishly. But, in spite of all her efforts at memorizing suitable social sentences and taming her heavy Polish accent, adjusting her taste in clothes and curling her hair less tightly, she failed to diminish her husband's growing irritation with her. More and more she stayed at home, going out only to the Polish National Church near her home on Sundays and other necessary days, and to shop, always alone, gathering groceries through narrow aisles, trying not to collide with the assured young American wives jabbering to each other as they shopped side by side. Always she felt herself a curiosity, a figure of fun. She hated to shop. She never knew that she was laughed at because, as she made her way through the aisles, she talked constantly to herself, fluently, quietly, nodding her head in reply, sometimes shaking it in negation to her own suggestions.

When Liza was born, Sterling bought a house on the East Side of the city. It was a small Cape Cod bungalow, compact, convenient and inexpensive, with a miniscule lawn in front and a garage where a garden might have been in the rear. It suited Sterling perfectly. He was gone most of the week on a route throughout the state, and he liked to come home to complete freedom from household and gardening chores. To Lena, used to the warmth of the lush Iowa farm, it seemed a pallid and constricted life. Sleeping in a twin-sized bed, working over an apartment-sized kitchen sink and stove built, it seemed to her, for a midget, squeezed under the corner-confines of a built-in dinette table at which, for lack of a dining room, they ate all their meals, Lena thought of life as a perpetually corsetted phenomenon, drained of all color and heat. She felt like the solitary prisoner in the ancient Chinese torture, locked in a box just a little too small for her to stand erect, too narrow to bend an arm or leg.

Only in church—and she chose later to go across the city by bus to the West Side's Cathedral, a great imitation European-Gothic structure of soaring arches and vast interior—and in Mr. Herman Schultz's corner grocery, which she adopted after Sterling had stopped driving her to the supermarket, did she feel entirely at home. Mr. Schultz spoke German, she could understand almost every word and could feel an old, nostalgic warmth during his long, involved gutteral sentences. Clerks in department stores embarrassed her with their stares, and so she made all her own clothes, cutting them on the cellar floor and then sewing them up on an old machine her father had given her as a wedding present.

But she had never recovered from her deep sense of gratitude to Sterling for marrying her and giving her a child, and so she never complained, although she suffered constantly from a sense of physical and emotional strangulation. Sterling, freed of her irritating public presence, was home very seldom now. So it was not until Liza was thirteen and fully grown, aware of the strange gulf between her parents but unable to understand its cause, that Sterling realized exactly what Liza's existence meant to him.

In that year Liza stopped going across the city every Sunday and went to church with her father. She enjoyed the new feeling of pride in her worshipping partner, who matched her so perfectly: coming out of church with him, she could feel the congregation looking at them admiringly. Little by little he formed the habit of coming home before noon on Saturday after five days on the road, changing his clothes and then taking Liza with him on his few local calls. They would lunch together at a roadside stand and then go to a movie in the afternoon. Because her sixteenth birthday coincided with his yearly vacation, they spent it together at Clear Lake, swimming, boating, going to movies and eating their meals at tables at the back of barrooms. The weather was so fine that they stayed on for three extra days, without notifying Lena, who waited a day and then ate the birthday cake she had baked for Liza's return.

A year later, because by now they looked so much of an age, she a mature young girl and he a youthful older man who seemed to meet at an exact point between the distance and so to neutralize it, at one of their barroom dinners he ordered her her first drink. It had the added delight of being surreptitious since you could order a drink in Des Moines only if the bartender knew you well and if the Legislature was not meeting in town at the moment. Now their partnership was complete. He took her everywhere he went. In the summer, on his trips to Cedar Rapids, Kansas City, Davenport, they stayed at motels, sharing a suitcase and for economy sharing a room, signing the register Elizabeth and Sterling Rankin.

If Lena, left behind in her solitary, cabined existence, objected to the curious loneliness of her life or the even more curious, exclusive companionship of theirs she never spoke of it to them or to anyone else. Her voice bottled up in her throat just as her body was confined within her coffin of a house, she rarely spoke except to herself and to God, from whom she nightly demanded an explanation for her exile, and from whom she seemed to receive no answer. As she grew older, the open, simple soul within the undistinguished frame became bitter, with a black inner rot such as a tomato develops when it hangs on a vine that receives no water. Her conversations with herself became abrupt ejaculations, muttered denials. While her husband and her daughter lunched and dined together at little places on the road, or danced at the Dealers' parties, she crouched on the little padded stool in her bedroom, reading the prayers under "Miscellaneous" at the back of her Polish Missal, considering what they would be doing now on the Dubuque farm, her close, warm brothers who matched her in strangeness, and her aging father who had retired and now sat on his porch watching his sons farm. She cared little for what she wore but curiously enough always spent some time each morning debating amid her large collection of earrings about which pair to wear. She would change at noon and again at dinner time, as if the periodically exchanged jewelry served to mark the passage of time which otherwise would flow on with inexorable sameness.

At the University Liza missed her father, and he almost went mad with loneliness for her. He drove his car as if it were a sweating, foaming horse down to Iowa City each week end, no matter where on his route Friday found him, and went home to Lena only when Liza came home on holidays. Still wearing his boyhood on his face, his square, straight shoulders encased in a white evening jacket, his brown hair intact and cut short, he took Liza to the Junior Prom, then to the Senior Prom. She wore his beautiful flowers proudly, straightened his plaid bow tie, admired the matching cummerbund, and introduced him all around as "Sterling." Whether this was his first or last name nobody knew and nobody thought to ask.

In all this time Liza had never realized that her father had, in every sense but the literal, taken her as his wife. She adored him, she found no one to equal his charm, his looks, his light-hearted, gently protective gallantry, his ease with cars and clothes and money. Beside him the University boys seemed gauche and childish. For long stretches of time she almost forgot her mother's existence, for Sterling was father and mother, brother and suitor to her, and when she remembered to ask, "How's Mother?" he would shrug and say, "All right," making an offhand *moue* as if even the thought of Lena should reduce them both to an attitude of tolerant amusement.

After graduation Liza lived for a year in Des Moines, not at home but in a small flat near Drake University. She worked fitfully on her master's degree in education, saw a great deal of her father who would hear of nothing but that he still pay all her expenses. Strangely enough, even now, Liza, small boned and still glowing with the complexion of a redhead, her hair seemingly still with a life of its own, never became interested in any of her male classmates who, intrigued by her looks and her remoteness, futilely sought her out. Perhaps because of his sufficiency to her; perhaps because she sensed how difficult it would be to establish an extra-paternal relationship; however it was, she continued along the same paths her life had taken since she was thirteen. *In time,* she thought, *he will let me go and then I will be free to* . . . But he never did, voluntarily. And then, while he sat in the bleachers at the Drake Field House watching Liza march in an endless line of black-robed candidates for degrees, Lena Rankin hung herself from the top rail of the stall shower in her bungalow. Ironically she had almost missed what she so ardently sought. During her final agonies the rail had broken loose from the wall, and when Sterling found her she had fallen to the tile floor, her head beyond the bathroom door, as if, even during her last mortal act, the space into which his bungalow-sized concept of existence had condemned her had not been adequate to hold the entire body and spirit of Lena Rankin.

His wife's death inwardly touched Sterling very little. After a short time, during which he disposed of everything that had belonged to her, giving Liza the only things of value, her little collection of silver earrings from Poland, and having had the damage to the bathroom wall and fittings repaired, he asked Liza to move back into the East Side bungalow with him. For the first time in their long friendship, she refused. He was deeply hurt because he could not comprehend the depths of her sense of guilt, her despair for her future in the light of what had just happened, her astonishment at her own selfishness and blindness, and her feeling that, in her inexcusable ignorance, she had committed an irrevocable sin against her mother and her mother's forgotten Catholic God.

Twenty years later Elizabeth Rankin (after her mother died she dropped the "Liza" and never told anyone that it had ever been her name) was still unreconciled to her part in her mother's death. She never married (perhaps because in a sense she *had* been married for so many years), and she turned violently against the avenues of forgiveness and penance that she remembered were present in her mother's church: she was to despise Catholics and Catholicism for the rest of her life. She confined her hair, now almost entirely gray on the top and ends, into a tight, unremitting bun, and the flesh on her face and neck fell back to reveal the tenuous fibers and knotted cords behind it. Now, perhaps because the catafalque on which her neurasthenic body was constructed dominated the soft flesh fastened to it, she emanated a sense of absolute control, as if her movements, decisions and actions were regulated as fully and completely as her flesh and hair. Wherever control could be gained, she sought it. She could not bear to see disorganization which to her was soft, permissive and dangerous. She feared that the failure to foresee and organize and plan would free events to take their own calamitous course as they had on that terrible May day in Iowa, to escape control and thus to threaten her whole existence with chaos. Unknown to her, the Scurvy Elephant Society held as one of its tenets that she owned a rubber stamp saying *Spectanda Est* which she placed on the record of every girl of whom she had the least suspicion, and that this was fully two thirds of the student body. But it was not entirely so; if Elizabeth Rankin in her lifelong condemnation of what she herself had done was watching anyone suspiciously it was herself, and only after a constant check, like a prison warden making night rounds of beds with a flashlight, did she turn her thus diminished distrust upon the faculty and the girls.

Sterling and Elizabeth rarely saw each other again. Like conspirators who have brought off a robbery successfully and then agree to share the takings and separate, they seemed to feel that contact would incriminate them. They sent Hallmark cards on their birthdays and at Christmas, feeling safe enough behind the printed messages. Elizabeth heard that he had become a trustee of his church and active on the school board, but she never left New England to see him, and he never came East to see her. It was as if they wished to lessen their mutual load of guilt by permanently dividing it into two parts.

Her mother's box of earrings remained on her dresser, augmented by the ones she bought regularly and added to the collection. Now she returned the pair she had been wearing to its place on the rack, chose another that matched the clean blouse she had just put on and blindly screwed them on to her ears. She felt her freshly reconstructed bun for completeness, looked at her watch, and went out.

The faculty lounged in chairs at the rear of the auditorium. The great room was the crowning touch to the new Arts Hall, built two years ago as a result of a strenuous building campaign among parents, alumnae and the Board of Governors. It was a wide, featureless room with a stage at one end and a massive picture window at the back. Its modernity was somehow depressing; the walls on both sides, entirely without fenestration, were lined with wide strips of a treated wood. Intended to give the room an illusion of height, the device succeeded only in making its inhabitants feel caged, "penned in," Robbie Parks called it. The auditorium itself stood at the apex angle of a building shaped like a hollow triangle, its three painfully equal sides consisting of classrooms enclosing a courtyard not yet under any discernible cultivation. The architect, whose mother had attended Miss Hands in the days when classrooms were still housed in a spacious, erratic and charming Victorian building, had in mind when he designed the structure a total absence of excess space and no wasted areas. This blatant simplicity had had no effect whatever on its cost, but it had eliminated from the finished building all the cubbyholes, all the secret places, the great ancient closets and stair-well cubicles that older buildings like the Faculty House and Elias Cook Hall still retained, and which so delighted students looking for privacy or solitude.

Last year, after their first, proud tour of the new Hall, this characteristic of pure utility was noticed by the students who were always alert to places where they might escape the official eye. The building was then immortalized by one student, now "gone on" in the normal process of events, who pointed out, "You know, Joe Louis once said about a fellow he was going to fight: 'he can run but he can't hide.' Wait till you see. That's the sort of building you can try running in but there's absolutely no place to hide."

It was true. The triangle terminated in two major exits. Miss Blount's office guarded one, Miss Rankin's the other, and only the faculty room, a small fish bowl of a room of which two walls were entirely glass—"a corner room for the cornered" it had been called—offered any retreat to teachers during the long, arid day of teaching. The students had none, except the toilet rooms. All day they were mercilessly exposed to a glaring world of brick and glass and bare white walls, all meeting each other at incorruptible angles, the corridors connecting them straight and undeviating, the turns abrupt and exact. Modern school architecture, to the residents of Miss Hands, was a triumph of observers over the observed. Trudy Langer once suggested that the words *Spectanda Est* be engraved over the entering doorways as a substitute for the old motto, suggested it, that is, to the charter members of the Scurvy Elephant Society.

No one had stirred in the faculty row at the back of the auditorium. Mr. James, wearing a striped sports jacket, light green shirt and off-white bow tie, sat at the piano near the front, idly picking out the Processional Hymn. Mr. James was what Miss Blount referred to, at Mothers' Meetings, as *Our Maestro*. He was middle-aged, lived a mile away from the school with his wife and daughter, and like Millicent, "came in" three days a week to play for Chapel, give music classes and a few private lessons. Today his annoyance could be sensed clearly by the fact that he played and replayed a hymn he had used almost daily for the last five years. He was no man for change and experimentation, and he rarely felt comfortable with a new hymn.

Miss Blount came up the stage steps, leaning forward from the waist, anxious for a few moments at the lectern before the students . . .

"One moment, please, Mr. James. I haven't found my reading yet."

Mr. James was the faculty's only male. He knew well the strength of his position, age-old and needing no definition, and furthermore he was annoyed at having been called in on a Saturday to play for the extra Chapel. He went on with his tentative playing, brushing the keys with his finger tips.

Miss Blount lifted the heavy half of the Bible over with both hands. She bent her head over the page, straightened and then turned the pages again. It was not, Ellen thought, watching her from the back row, that she was searching for new passages of fresh wisdom: inevitably she would settle for Ecclesiastes 3, 1–9, or the 24th Psalm or, in a real pinch, the words of Ruth to Naomi. But the effect of the daily search through the pages of the great book was thought by the Headmistress to be this: that having looked widely one fell back always upon the best, Ecclesiastes 3, 24th Psalm, Ruth to Naomi. . . .

Miss Blount settled the Bible on the lectern and moved her hands up to settle her hair, her efforts with the heavy Bible having dislocated a number of strands. She took off her glasses, put them into her hair at the top of her head and looked to the back row of chairs.

"Ladies, shall we stand for the Processional?"

The faculty stood up, reaching behind them to place their books, papers and newspapers on their seats. Miss Moore stood straight, bracing her shoulders against some invisible force. Mrs. Bache's shoulders rounded as she strained toward the podium; her hearing was slowly diminishing and her body, stretched toward the speaker, formed a shell to catch whatever sound might come. Her arms strained under the load of texts she held in front of her. She seemed to hope that by her posture she was demonstrating her extreme eagerness to listen. The Twins stood together, their knuckles barely touching, staring straight ahead but aware only of each other. Madame Mifflin dutifully held her hymnal open before her although the number of the Processional had not yet been announced. Ellen stood leaning on the chair in front of her, full of resentment at having to put down James Reston and the review of V. S. Pritchett's new book. Meg Miers twirled a ball-point pen in her fingers; abstractedly considering the forms made by her fingers and the long rod. Miss Seward had not yet arrived.

"What's the Processional?" asked the Headmistress.

"Four Thirty-Three," replied Mr. James. While Miss Blount began her feverish riffling through the pages of her hymnal, he went to the door of the auditorium. Stretched down through the corridor of Arts Hall as far as he could see were two straggly rows of students. A steady hum, punctuated by occasional laughter, rose from them, like morning fog from low-lying bushes. Between the rows moved Miss Rankin, her voice low and insistent, counting students off according to the rows of seats they were about to occupy.

A sophomore student suddenly appeared in the middle of one attenuated line, having emerged from a bathroom at the upper end of the Hall. Miss Rankin's voice began its abrupt ascent at once, shocking the students nearest her into silence.

"Now you've thrown off the whole count. What can you be thinking of? Where do you properly belong?" Her voice shrilled; the student looked ready to cry.

"Here . . . I think, Miss Rankin."

"Are you in the upper half of the alphabet?"

Wildly the student, whose name was Lorimer, started to count on her fingers buried in the pockets of her jeans.

"Yes, no . . . yes, I mean, Miss Rankin."

"Then you belong in the other line and in place according to height, tall at the back."

"Parade rest," whispered Trudy to the girl in front of her who had suddenly begun to slump in order to appear shorter than Trudy.

Miss Lorimer, now completely confused about the location of both her name and her height, stumbled across the aisle and inserted herself behind a girl taller than she.

"Wrong," screamed Miss Rankin, her face red with fury. "Can't you see you're wrong? Move, move, move . . ." and taking the arm of the befuddled girl she shot her roughly into line at the proper place.

Miss Rankin's voice had reached its zenith and broke, returned to its normal posture as if to recoup its energies for the next precipitious rise, like a mountain climber returning to base camp to rest before a new assault upon the summit. To the students Miss Rankin's voice was a weapon not unlike a gun in the hands of a madman. It threatened danger to them should they come within its unreasoning range; even worse, it terrified them by suggesting, in its tremors and breaks, its sharp rises, ringing top note and sudden calms, some subconscious dislocation in its owner. They were more frightened of seeing her crack before their eyes than of being the object of her anger. Dimly they sensed that she was her own victim, and they were wary of being present at her self-immolation.

Echoes of the excitement in the corridor reached the waiting faculty, shifting their feet in the rear row. They listened, trying to make out what was causing the noise, although they knew well that lining up the School and counting them off into equal lines according to height and class and alphabetical standing always reduced Miss Rankin to a state. She insisted on doing the job alone—indeed, any suggestion, no matter how helpful, always increased her fury, for she was immediately suspicious of its intent and lumped it together with other subversive acts, like inattention, disobedience and muddleheadedness, as deliberate attempts to frustrate her careful plans.

The heat in the corridor grew worse. Students, red-faced and damp, were obliging each other by pulling wet shirts away from the backs of the girls in front of them. The odor of hot feet in much-used sneakers rose from the tile floor.

"Straighten those lines, *and be still*," screamed Miss Rankin, catching, as she walked down past Trudy Langer and Emily Courtney, the odor of tobacco smoke. This will be dealt with later in the morning, she said grimly to herself, once we have finished with this. Miss Rankin's moods were of two orders. There were those which broke at once, like fragile china at the first knock, and those she extended, by the force of her considerable will, to a later date of maturation. The faculty knew that her delayed rages were the worst, like a storm which gathers force slowly and breaks with greater force because of its long self-containment.

At the doors to the auditorium she came upon Mr. James. He leaned against the jamb, his hand in his long, thick, black hair, befitting his role of Maestro, his face stony against the inner amusement he was feeling. To him all feminine displays of control were only unconvincing pretenses. He loved to catch Miss Rankin in one of her rages. Her demeanor toward him had always been that of a collected, silent woman. He was too dull-witted, perhaps too self-involved, to realize the true nature of her quiet moods: actually, like a foresighted squirrel against winter need, she was constantly storing up evidence to be presented in some future case. In this mood she ignored the present pleasures of action in favor of future feasts of revenge. Only now and then, under the pressures of heat or weariness, or the unbearable cumulative evidence of the stupidity of every human creature around her, did she explode as she had just done.

"The Processional is Four Thirty-Three," he said to her.

"Four Thirty-Three," said Miss Rankin, managing to make the numbers ring through the fetid corridor like a whip.

"Lead us O Father in the paths of peace," sang the first, short girls, stepping off into the auditorium. Mr. James pounded the chords hard, almost drowning out the feeble tones of students who were trying simultaneously to keep pace, read the words in their hymnals and find the right row of seats to enter.

The faculty stood wearily, feeling the heat settle upon them from the unprotected picture windows at their backs. Madame Mifflin, full of an audible Protestant ardor which the sight of the Episcopal hymnal always aroused in her, was singing, a little off key, a corrupt version of the hymn, filtering its Anglican sentiments through the sieve of her French accent. Ellen listened to her, being silent herself, and considering Madame's rendition of Four Thirty-Three a real and welcome detriment to the cause of the Reformation.

Robbie whispered to Jo: "Your hair's still wet. Why do you have to wash it in this beastly heat?"

Jo shrugged and did not answer. She was wondering where Sophie was. Mrs. Bache shifted from one foot to the other. She was tired: her legs had never regained their strength after years of standing in lines most of the day and half the night for food and admittance to the latrine. Now she could only think of sitting down again.

"And doubts appall, and sorrows still increase . . ." sang Trudy Langer, marching without her hymnal. Just ahead of her Patty Lorimer extended her confusion by starting up the wrong row of seats.

"Wrong, wrong, *wrong*," Miss Rankin rushed out of the doorway where she had been observing the progress of the marchers. Thoroughly aroused, nothing could now stay the Assistant Headmistress's fury. Propelled by it she rushed to the row Lorimer had mistakenly entered.

"Back. Move back. We'll do it all again, and I personally shall escort Miss Lorimer to her correct place."

Back to the corridor trudged the students, their hymnals lowered. Mr. James stopped playing and sat stolidly at the piano, his hanging arms, he hoped, a vivid and silent testimony to his distaste for the whole proceeding.

"This is not a rout. It's a strategic retreat," muttered Trudy to Emily.

"When are you going to put the key back?" asked Emily.

"Silence," shrilled Miss Rankin, following the last students to the door. A sullen quiet fell over the army reassembling in the corridor.

Miss Blount, still standing at the lectern, was also silent. She glanced furtively at the faculty, whose bent heads and half-turned backs indicated their disgust. She made a show of turning the Bible and then returned doggedly to her pursuit of vagrant bits of gray hair. A long silence filled the auditorium. When the Processional still did not pick up, she walked quickly to the control panel at the side of the stage and shut off the auditorium lights. For a moment she paused, thinking she detected a slight odor of tobacco smoke, sniffed at the wall, decided she must be mistaken and returned to her place.

"Too hot for all that illumination," she said, by way of explanation to Mr. James who was, literally, at her feet under the stage.

Save a buck: thought Mr. James.

Ellen: *I won't be able to read a word now.*

Mrs. Bache: *Perhaps now she won't see if I sit.*

Jo: *I wonder where Sophie is.*

"All right, Mr. James. Again, please," called Miss Rankin.

"Without thy guiding hand we go astray," sang the returning first regiment.

Madame's voice, alone in its ardor joined in: "Lead us through Christ, the true and living Way."

The end of the lines was now in sight. Miss Rankin joined Patty Lorimer and gestured her conspicuously into the right row. Patty struck her foot against a chair in embarrassment, gave Miss Rankin a look of pure hatred but made her passage to her seat without further incident. The students, all in place now, stood, singing the descant of the hymn. Miss Rankin nodded to Miss Blount, who had been anxiously watching for a sign, and then joined the faculty in the back row.

Mr. James played a chord. The school sat, Mrs. Bache being the first down. Lucy Moore sat precisely as the note sounded. Bemused by a daydream that had suddenly assailed her, Ellen was the last down. Then she had to rise slightly to pull the *Times* out from under her. She caught Miss Blount's disapproving eye as she once again sat down.

But Miss Blount had seen it done by Miss Rankin and took strength from it. She was on her feet at once.

"Girls, we *must* do this sitting in unison. It looks perfectly terrible from up here, straggling down to your seats. Let's try sitting again. Mr. James, please."

Mr. James played a chord. The school rose wearily.

"And girls, when you sit, will everyone please take their feet off the chair in front."

Ellen winced. Robbie looked over and gave Ellen a reassuring wink. They all sat, and stood, and sat again, and then, satisfied by the repetition although there was no outward evidence that the last trial was any better than the first, the Headmistress began the reading:

"To everything there is a season, and a time to every purpose . . ." Sighing at the familiar opening the audience settled
itself to think of other things. Miss Blount's Old Testament
readings were comforting in this respect: her fidelity to the
few texts she had known since childhood was absolute—they
had been her father's favorites as well—and this permitted the
school a few free moments of planning or dreaming or near-
sleep. Over their unhearing but solemnly bent heads droned
the familiar words:

". . . under the heaven: a time to be born and time to die;
a time to plant, and a time to pluck up that which is . . ."

Sophie crouched over the wicker coffee table in the Faculty
Room at the other end of Arts Hall. She had heard, distinctly,
some echoes of the scene in the corridor, the pounding of feet
out and then in again and then out again of the corridor. Each
time there was a silence she had risen and gone to the door, but
the lash of Rankin's voice, although she couldn't distinguish
the words, cutting through the corridor stopped her from going
to the auditorium. Now she sat over the miniscule warmth of
a cigarette burning before her in the ash tray, adding its mite
to the room's insufferable heat. Two entire walls of the Faculty
Room were glass: through them the sun poured in undisturbed.
Like an aboriginal bush boy warming himself over his single
burning brand, Sophie huddled around her cigarette, absorbed
in its ash.

The martial sounds of Elgar drifted through the door. Suddenly it was opened and Madame came in swiftly to sit close
to Sophie on the couch. Having adequately established her
presence at Chapel by singing prominently, she had then left
by the back door as soon as practice for Commencement singing had started. Descants and parts-singing always confused
her, her own ear being attuned to only one harmonic path at
a time.

She lit a cigarette. Sophie's mail lay on the table. Putting her match away, Madame's sleek little black eyes saw at once that two or three of her letters were standard communications from publishers ("Is Written Expression bothering your Junior Classes? Send for our guaranteed workbooks with, of course, separate teacher Answer Booklets . . ."). One envelope, torn open, bore the return address of the Dworkin Summer Institute.

"Have you yet heard from the summer school?" asked Madame, now ignoring the pile of mail and looking at Sophie with her professional look of deep concern.

Sophie had followed her eyes. Caring not at all, and too weary and hot even to be indignant, she merely spoke the truth:

"I have. No soap. They've had a full staff since February and no resignations lately, or anything of that sort."

"I am so sorry." And then quickly, because she couldn't help herself: "What will you do now?"

"I don't know."

"May I ask—have you thought of a Bureau?"

"I have thought of just about everything. But my previous record, as they say in police movies, with the Teachers Bureau in Boston is not very good. I'm like an accident-prone driver applying for insurance. They don't consider me a very good risk, I'm afraid. At the moment my greatest worry is money . . ." Sophie had almost forgotten Madame's presence and was thinking aloud to herself. "If I could borrow enough to hold out through the summer . . . I owe a great deal on the loan I took last June to hold me for the summer . . . and a few time payments that I still need to make. . . ."

Sophie went on, unconscious that she was providing the avid little Frenchwoman beside her with conversational sustenance for some time to come. Madame listened deeply and made comforting, deeply accented clucking noises. Sophie described the bank's growing impatience with her uneven payments, she hinted at an earlier loan from a bank in New York which was not quite paid up. Whimsically she mentioned the payments remaining on the Douay:

"Can you imagine the ceremony that would be involved in reclaiming a Bible? Boys carrying candles and incense, black-robed acolytes—it *is* a Catholic version, you know." Sophie smiled at her fancy, but her hand shook as she tried to grind out her cigarette. The strain of her outburst of humor showed in her face.

"I could lend you a little, perhaps fifty dollars. If that would help you?" Madame leaned forward, delightedly contemplating herself embarked on a future narrative: the little Miss Seward had worked upon her sympathies, so nervous. . . . Then she had skipped out owing her fifty dollars. The position it would give her from which to begin next year! Generous. Too trusting (Mrs. Bache would say this). The heroine of the whole sorry mistake in hiring. Miss Blount should have seen from the first . . . But I could not help but feel sorry . . . how she shook. Already Madame felt repaid in interest, attention, for the loan.

Once over her delicious daydream Madame's deep frugality considered Sophie's situation with horror. To become an economic victim, unable to rise, to fail to plan ahead, to lose control over one's possessions: all these things violated her passion for absolute ownership.

"But you must not allow yourself to become discouraged. I must tell you about my daughter's first appointment after her graduation. You will be most interested in this. Despite her excellent European education she was forced—things were very bad in Europe after the War—to begin as a clerk and to work among persons much inferior to her in breeding and in training. Until one day when she met . . ."

Well launched into another in the vast apochrypha of tales which by now surrounded her son and daughter in the minds of the faculty, stories of their inimitable European existence, their unparalleled educations and their glamorous love lives which included both highly placed marriages and clean, beautiful extra-marital affairs, even, it was remembered, a significant encounter with Jacqueline Bouvier at the Sorbonne when she and the ubiquitous Dorothea Lukacs-Mifflin had been students there, Madame droned on and on, happily embroidering upon her dreams, largely unaware of her listener. Madame believed sincerely that when she said "you will be interested in this" her audience could not help but be caught by the enchantment in which she herself basked. The force of her tales was great enough entirely to compel her; she could not conceive of anyone being able to resist their centripetal pull.

The story of Dorothea's gallant victory over a Fate which would have kept her degraded as a clerk wore on. Sophie had long since stopped listening. She had returned to her private world in which lack of any money at all, the letter saying no summer job, the increasing vagueness of a teaching job for next fall, debts, and a sense of failure at Miss Hands all formed a knotted, gritty tangle.

"Will it help you?" The question broke in upon Sophie's jungle-retreat. The long anecdote had come to an end. They were back at the offer.

"It would help, yes. I'm grateful to you." Vaguely she remembered saying this before today. She recognized in the words a sign that she had begun the last phase of her yearly struggle away from all the places she had been: stranded and enervated, she was now, in her fantasy, sitting on a roof entirely surrounded by the flood waters of her mistaken choices. She could see small boats from every direction on the shore setting out to help her. At this moment, in the heat of this unbearable Saturday, with the memory of the last night's scorn, and the words said in the faculty sitting room—and the long rip in the ancient black curtain—she found herself unable to measure her total disaster, for she could see only the immediate and temporary stopgaps offered her: the Cape for a week, fifty dollars. "At least it will quiet the collector who is handling my Bible account," she said to Madame.

"I think I'd better slip back now. She always knows when you are not there but never when you are."

"What are they doing?"

"Rehearsing for Commencement and for that Parents' Processional."

"I don't think I'll go in. There's nothing they need me for. And I hate to look at that rip those high-spirited little dears made in the rear curtain last night. Four feet long. I taped it together, but in this heat it can't hold together long. She'll see it."

"Is not it so? Those curtains are from the old building. I warned about them. They are very old." Madame could not resist her need to emphasize to the transient Sophie her own permanence at Miss Hands, as well as her sibyl-knowledge that was always, to "their" later dismay, ignored. But her voice still managed to retain its full measure of sympathy for Sophie's predicament.

"They are indeed. But the Headmistress told me, when I once said I thought they were going, that they were *expected* to last."

"Nothing lasts, but here everything is expected to." Madame felt pleased at her ability to philosophize and decided to leave on that personally satisfactory note.

Alone, Sophie gathered up her mail. *Fifty dollars against the animosity of the Universe, a nail against the Himalayas.* Strains of Elgar came from behind the still-shut doors of the auditorium. As she arrived at the doors they swung into her face. She was sent back against the wall by tall seniors walking in the stately, pomp-and-circumstance Recessional, making their escape from the rehearsal. Trudy Langer stared at Sophie as she passed. Sophie looked down, her head nodding to Elgar, her chin striking her chest.

The faculty tail-end of the Recessional passed Sophie: "Savior, again to thy dear Name we raise with one accord our parting hymn of praise . . ." Ellen smiled at her.

"Cheer up. There'll be another show Monday. Same time, same stars."

Jo came up to her, lagging behind Robbie who seemed not to notice Sophie and walked on. Jo stopped.

"What happened to you?"

"I waited for my mail. No luck. I can go to the Cape with you any time, Mr. Samuel W. Dworkin regretfully informs me."

"That's fine," said Jo. Her pleasure was real, the pleasure of an isolated member of a large, happy family beginning to gather people around her again, to recreate the warmth engendered by many people assembled together voluntarily. "I'll tell Robbie. See you at lunch."

"Yes. I'm going to try to do something about those black curtains."

Ellen overheard. She had seen the sabotage during the play. "The Saints preserve you as they have those curtains all these many years," she said. "I think I'll improve the next shining hour by locking horns with Comments. I ought to be able to compose some pretty telling truths on those damned juniors in an hour."

Ellen moved toward the Faculty Room, Sophie went into the now-deserted auditorium. Silence and heat were left in full possession of the east corridor.

Inserting a half-sheet of carbon paper between two sheets of a Comment pad, Ellen wrote:

"Marcia has worked hard. Only her weakness in the technical aspects of English prevents her from achieving a higher grade. D+." She signed her name on the line designated Teacher, and tore two comment sheets off the pad.

Having written the first of her sixty-seven comments that were required by the School to accompany report cards at the end of each half, Ellen sat back and contemplated it. After she had done the first few she felt she had almost finished, but at the tenth or eleventh she was suddenly appalled by the distance she had still to go.

. . . *"weakness in the technical aspects of the language"*: *euphemism for cannot spell, punctuate or construct a simple declarative sentence, especially confectioned to make facts more palatable for high-tuition-paying parents.* . . .

Now that one was finished her mood had darkened. She wrote:

"Evelyn's showing on the College Boards and on objective testing at mid-semester was poor, but her class work indicates she is an interested, attentive and courteous student. C—"

And then:

"Lucia has shown considerable improvement in her writing this quarter, but her reading comprehension still needs work. A summer course in rapid reading and comprehension . . ."

Ellen crossed out the last sentence quickly, remembering too late the admonition at the last faculty meeting against this kind of comment. Miss Blount felt strongly that any indication of a need for outside help cast dangerous aspersions upon the completeness of Miss Hands's preparation of its girls for all possible academic trials and any conceivable future.

She crumpled Lucia Engle's comment and began on a clean sheet. Lucy Moore came out of the bathroom, her arms full of class rolls and comment pads.

"God, it's that time again," she said, flopping down beside Ellen. Ellen nodded sympathetically: "I've done three, and I've said all I have to say on the subject of my semiliterate juniors."

"The ideal comment," said Lucy, "is one which says 'Ability: fair. Accomplishment: nil. C.'" As she sat and talked, she had already ripped off three comments based on this stated ideal.

"I have an ideal comment but I've never had the nerve to write it: 'There is no substitute for native intelligence.'" Ellen doodled, tore off another sheet and aimed it at a wastebasket across the room.

"That's very good," said Lucy appreciatively, praising both the successful shot and the good comment in one phrase, "but it takes too many words. My system involves four words and a minor amount of punctuation. It has infinite variety and combinations. I never say 'Ability: Nil,' however. That would be contrary to Miss Blount's theory that *every* rich girl has ability, *ipso facto*. And as a matter of fact, in my subject it's quite true. They've all been riding and playing games since they were six. I'd say their ability was hereditary. It comes from inheriting ponies and tennis courts and sixteen-foot sailboats."

Ellen recognized the sacrifice that a speech of this length represented for Lucy. "I see what you mean. Too bad it doesn't carry over into English Literature. I could do with a few literate chromosomes to teach now and then."

Lucy braced her shoulders and went on scrawling her comments. "It's the physical act of writing I dislike. Once launched I hardly think about what I'm putting down. But my hand cramps and ruins my disposition—and my posture."

"When do you leave for Williams?"

"Not today, damn it. This extra Chapel ruined my plans. I've resigned myself to Comments and some tennis with Robbie later. A lost week end."

Ellen wrote: "Inattentive to details, frequent carelessness in preparation of homework, but her writing shows imagination and . . ."

"Ability: fair. Accomplishment: Fair. C," wrote Lucy.

Silence, composed of concentration, a determination to be charitable at the cost of truth, and heat, settled down over the Faculty Room.

Sadly Miss Blount gazed at the tattered black curtains.

"I think they can be sewn."

"I doubt it, Miss Blount. They're giving way at both sides of the rip, and at top and bottom. I really think they need replacing."

"But we shall try sewing them first, Miss Seward. I don't really think we can tell until we try." Miss Blount's voice took on its it-will-cost-money edge.

Sophie flushed at Miss Blount's insistent use of the pronoun, a carry-over, she thought from first-grade days: *Now, shall we put our blocks back on the shelves?*

"Jane's work occasionally reveals some awareness of the basic requirements of English prose but . . ."

"Ability: moderate. Accomplishment: Improving."

"Those curtains were almost completely ruined last night during the play. Have you seen them?"

Elizabeth Rankin had, when she had gone on the trail of a wisp of smoke she saw curling out from under the stage door, but she thought it wise to allow the indignant Headmistress full scope to describe them. Having listened with a show of absolute attention, she then said: "She's never had any sort of control over the girls. It should have been apparent to us from her record. We're fortunate she's leaving."

Miss Blount only vaguely understood the intent of the remark, so she did not reply. She was aware that Elizabeth Rankin's appetite for power was insatiable, and she was aware too, although she did not understand why, that it was possible to feed it fully and still keep her in her role as assistant. The reason for this was too subtle for Miss Blount's elementary powers of human understanding. For Miss Rankin needed to dominate as she needed to breathe. Attached to this primary need was a secondary one: to be universally recognized to be the source of power and permissions, all arrangements and decisions, while at the same time serving under a universally acknowledged-to-be incompetent Headmistress. In this satisfying relationship she knew it was said by the rest of the faculty that Miss Blount was a figurehead, that all questions could only be decisively settled with Rankin, and at the same time, that the Headmistress could not hold her job without her. The delicacy of this relation required that Miss Rankin hold every position of authority in the School: she was Head of the Academic Department, Guidance Director, Director of Admissions, Permanent Chairman of the Honor Society, Director of Curriculum, in charge of the Schedule, Secretary of the Disciplinary Committee. To share these responsibilities would be to weaken her secondary vision of herself as the sole support of a decaying structure. It would be as if a single great king post, holding up the center point of a gable roof without benefit of struts, were to be replaced with a series of small, efficient metal pieces, each lending its strength to the rooftree. Elizabeth Rankin could survive in no social architecture except as king post; the rooftree position she left, by her own decision, to the aging Headmistress.

One vital job still eluded Miss Rankin's grasp: the hiring of the staff. Her statement about Sophie Seward was a part of a long-range campaign to indicate to the Headmistress, slowly and without pressure, that her own continued security depended upon the ultimate transfer of this final power to her assistant. Sophie was her entering wedge. But the Headmistress, relying upon what had always been her one strength, her instinctive sympathy for human beings (which in turn did seem to sustain them in moments of crisis) would not relinquish her last bastion of choice.

Miss Rankin repeated: "Six teaching posts in seven years. We should have known." This time Miss Blount was conscious of the intent of the plural pronoun. She smiled.

"Well, we needn't worry about that. I had a request for a recommendation for her from a school in New Hampshire. I plan to write quite frankly. And the new woman I've hired seems very capable. A Vassar graduate. Years of experience at Alvirah Scott and returning to teaching after raising a family. A widow. We'll have her daughter in the freshman class. She has a master's in library science, I think she said it was."

A number of Miss Hands's faculty had, at one time or another, come to teach in this way. Miss Blount kept a small, private file of the names of women, graduates of the Seven Sisters colleges (as she termed them), some of them alumnae of Miss Hands, with daughters either at Miss Hands already, or of an age to attend should it be made possible. Usually recently widowed, the economics of living at the school and educating their daughter or daughters at the same time, even in the face of a minute salary (*and after all, where else can you teach with a liberal arts degree and not one education credit?*) appealed to them. Thus Miss Blount, for whom subject matter was always secondary to the name of the college, had once, before Sophie, been successful in filling the position of Junior English Mistress with a lady who had graduated sixteen years before from Smith with a major in Mathematics, and at another time had a Mrs. Berk, Bryn Mawr, Class of '31, who taught advanced French at Miss Hands, although she had done very well at college in physics and chemistry. Miss Blount liked to fill her yearly announcements of new faculty with desirable colleges after their names, as if some of their success at entry and graduation might be presupposed by inquiring parents to be transferable to their daughters.

But the Headmistress's assurance about the new teacher did not entirely satisfy Miss Rankin. She said nothing, but mentally resolved on a plan of action: to watch her closely for signs of independence and trouble making, for overt moves toward position, especially since the Headmistress was always very sympathetic to new teachers, finding their qualities always more appealing and valuable than those of the old staff. This honeymoon period was short but dangerous. During it Miss Rankin had found it necessary to wait quietly, alertly, ready to spring at the first sign that persisting favor might result in permanent trust or power. In truth she preferred the appointment of a poor and shaky teacher to a good, self-assured one, for all her peculiar, private emotional needs could be satisfied only by a victim; a capable woman would require more planning, more traps, a greater exercise of her very considerable and cabalistic powers of denigration.

"Very good," she said to the Headmistress. "I've comments to write this morning."

"Why yes," said the Headmistress, with the playful air of a queen to her spoiled favorite, "Get to work."

Madame had Meg Miers's ear. Usually Meg was alert enough to avoid her in time, to duck behind an easel or into the paint closet. But this morning Madame, in active, determined search of a listener, was ineluctable. Meg was cleaning brushes at the sink in the Studio. Through the glass door Madame's accurate black eyes had spotted her and marked her for her own. She went into the Studio carefully, with the air of a conspirator, closing the door behind her.

"Bettina's handicap is her poor and infrequent reading habits, combined with an insufficient grasp of the principles of grammar. However it can be said in regard to her progress this quarter that . . ."

Lucy had, unaccountably, run out of adjectives. Stymied for a moment she thought hard, then reread the pile of Comments she had already written. Happily she began again to write: Ability: fair . . ."

". . . how anyone can come to be so heavily in debt! You would not believe it. Two bank loans, and now she thinks of another to carry her through the summer! And you will be interested in this, *a Bible*, costing almost forty dollars. . . ."

Robbie, upon whom the announcement of the Recessional hymn had come too suddenly, had left her class lists and Comment pads on the seat behind her in the auditorium. After their cigarette together in the Faculty Room, Jo walked back with her to pick them up. In the presence of Lucy Moore and Ellen Acton their smoldering row had been kept under tight, uncomfortable control. Now it flared, like a forest fire taking breadth and height and force from a clearing among the trees. The great area of the auditorium gave scope to their hostility.

"You're just like my Aunt Jane. Every damned stray cat."

"Oh Robbie, she has no place to stay. What difference can it make to us?"

"To you. Not to *us*. We do everything with *them* all year. We live on their schedule, wait until they're asleep, answer their bells. After June fifth I think of the three months ahead as mine and yours, ours, not theirs, a change in person, a freedom from *them*. And then you ask her down."

"Just for a while, Rob. Not the whole summer. Just until she finds something or some other place to go."

Robbie looked at Jo's earnest boy's face, her curling hair lying damp on her forehead, with yearning and love. She knew her own love to be the basic force within her, whereas Jo's was part of a universal embrace which overflowed her preferences and reached out to anyone near her who needed it or laid claim to it. She could never make Jo understand that for her fulfillment required sole possession, that outsiders diminished and weakened her. Now, for explanation to Jo she substituted anger, hoping to cut Sophie away from them by making use of Jo's profound fear of a scene.

"Let her alone, Jo. She's no good to anyone. She's a born leech, she is liable to crack up—look at that awful palsy in her hands and her head—she's a hollow old maid who hangs on to anyone who will let her. You're a natural host for her variety of sucker. We'll never be rid of her if you let her come down."

Jo felt herself losing her footing, slipping backward before the storm in Robbie's low voice.

"Rob, it's my cabin too. I'd like to have her for just a short visit."

"Fine. Oh fine. You can have her. But not me. Not if you have her."

"Come now, Rob. You don't really mean that."

"I do indeed. Either the lily maid or me. Not both."

Like a runner who feels a rush of air as his opponent passes him in the stretch, Jo knew at that moment that she had lost. Robbie collected her papers. They walked together toward the doors. Just before they stepped out into the public air of the corridor, Robbie reached across and rubbed Jo's curls in a brotherly gesture of forgiveness. The rout was complete.

Behind the curtains of the stage, Sophie sat on the piano stool making deep stabs with a carpet needle and heavy thread at the rent black curtains, listening to the rise and fall, the approach and departure of the Twins' voices locked in argument. She made no move to betray her presence. The vibration of her hands hindered her work, and as she paused to wait for some measure of control over them she found herself quoting to the empty stage and the vast auditorium beyond the lines of Stephen Crane she had read to her sophomores a few days ago: "Later he saw that each weed was a singular knife. 'Well,' he mumbled at last, 'Doubtless there are other roads.'"

"Tennis, anyone?" asked Robbie, her neck bent around the Faculty Room door.

"Lovely idea. I'm for it." said Lucy. She stood up swiftly, in the way she had of moving simultaneously as her words announced her intention. Comment sheets slid to the floor. Ellen helped collect them.

"Have fun."

"Lucy Moore—ability: not so hot, but it's better than what I'm doing at this moment. See you at lunch, Ellen."

"If I live," said Ellen, shaking her Comment pad grimly as if to fan herself.

Left alone, Ellen felt herself at the mercy of the oversized picture window which seemed, with sun pouring through it, to be part of the generalized assault of heat upon her. In a sudden, curious counter-move she slipped down from the couch to the floor. It was cooler there, cut away by the couch's bulk from the glaring, lidless eye of the monster window. And at once, drowsy and warm, she was back in the house of her mother. Her brothers and sisters knelt on each side of her, her mother sat forward on the edge of a straight chair, in token for the kneeling she could no longer do, and led them in the recitation of their nightly prayers:

". . . is the fruit of thy womb Jesus . . ."

Ellen was sitting on the floor, a concession to her tender, seven-year-old knees, watching the face of her mother for meaningful pauses, for signs of weariness or sickness.

". . . now and at the hour of our death . . ."

Her brothers and sisters, six of them, recited in the perfect unison of long-practiced Catholic school children, so that the caesuras coincided and the pauses for breath were aligned. Their backs unmoving, their knees perfectly adjusted to the uncarpeted floor, they went on tonelessly praying aloud:

". . . for us sinners now . . ."

Ellen had never known her father. He had died of a fall from a scaffold when she was four. Two painted walls of the dining room—the other two still covered with a faded flower-print paper—were all that remained to Ellen as physical evidence that he had ever existed. Her mother referred to him always in the negative. She would point her chin up at the wall, her voice deep with typical Irish scorn for the male, and say: "And he'd never finish anything he started." His English origin offended her deeply, even after years of marriage and the years he had been dead but again, she could never bring herself to assert the fact. "He wasn't Irish," was all she told Ellen. About his death she was more charitable, invoking the Almighty as a preface: "God help him, he never did anything right and he died the same way." Two old Jews returning from their daily walk on Riverside Drive had helped carry the broken painter to the police car that took him to a hospital. One of them learned his address and went to see Mrs. Acton. From her window she took one look at his beard, his black skullcap, his oversized coat, and refused to leave her chair to talk to him. "Tell him I'm not well," she told the small, shocked Ellen to whom the kindly Jew had already given his terrible message, "and thank him for coming."

After the death of Elliot Acton Senior the Actons led a strongly parochial life. Together, as long as Mrs. Acton could manage the walk, they went to daily Mass at six, to the Wednesday evening novena to Saint Jude and to the Friday evening novena in honor of the Seven Sorrows of the Virgin Mary. They made, together, all the first Fridays. On holy days of obligation the eight of them, kneeling together, occupied half the small communion rail at St. James, and the old parishioners would smile to each other to see them, dressed in somber, interchangeable, nondescript clothes, their broad, common Irish faces aglow with pleasure from having received Communion, return to their pew, which they occupied entirely, and alone.

Mrs. Acton had the face of a doll. Her cheeks were round, red and full of a constant shine, her straight black hair, with the daily help of a hot iron, curled in half-crescents into her face. As she grew fatter her hair seemed to be insufficient for her ballooning features until finally, when her weight was so great that she could no longer stand easily, it merely seemed to outline her head, without covering it. In her grade-school years Ellen and her mother would bring up the rear of the family procession into the Church of Saint James, Ellen staying behind so that her Mother would not be alone in her slow, heaving progress down the street and up the steps into the Church. Her halt at the holy water font became the full stop of a gigantic mastodon. She seemed to settle as she stopped. Ellen would tug at her skirt and push gently against her for some time before her mother gathered all the slowly disassociating elements of her gross bulk and moved on down the aisle.

The children went to the St. James parochial school, the older ones to Cathedral High, a longer walk across town. Mrs. Acton paid no tuition, in deference to her status, and dressed her children entirely in clothing from the annual school rummage sale, where she paid nothing for her "purchases" made after the more desirable items had been sold. But her patience with hand-me-downs was infinite; in her ponderous way, she would sew and cut and change until the clothing became what she called serviceable, if not in any sense attractive.

From her earliest years with the Mercy nuns Ellen remembered how admiringly the Sisters spoke of the Acton family life. The word she heard most often used about them was "edifying," and for a long time she believed it meant unified and regular in their attendance at Church. She basked, in these years, in the universal approval of her mother, her family, the way they lived and the perfect parochial picture of Catholic family life they presented to the non-Catholic world outside. Fatherless, she came to believe that there was something infinitely superior and fortunate in her mother's having substituted God the Father, a good Catholic and perhaps even an Irishman who did everything right, for the erring, feckless and mortal reality of her mother's memory. "Exemplary" was another word she heard used about her family by the nuns and by Father Morley, the pastor who also taught her religion.

Ellen remembered her youth, adolescence and early maturity in terms of her mother's weight because it directly affected her ability to move about normally. Then too, there seemed to be a strange, ineffable relation between Mrs. Acton's physical size and her presence in religious activities, and the strength of her sons' devotion. It had been as if, while she still accompanied them, there could be no denying her and her insistence on their regularity. But even with her there the boys had already begun to daydream in their seats, to lean back resting their knees during most of the Mass, watching the shoulders and cocked heads of the girls in the front rows. After Mass the three of them would excuse themselves politely, kiss their mother and leave the girls to walk home with her. And when the day came—Ellen remembered she was in eighth grade—when the walk to the Church made her mother's breathing come thick and fast in her heavy throat, and an ugly, red rash of perspiration and heat covered her face and neck and she stayed home on her love seat and waited for Father Morley to bring Com-

munion to her as often as he could, the boys left home with
the girls for Mass and novenas and Lenten prayers on the
evenings of Ember days but rarely went on into the Church
with them.

Ellen's mother sat at home, reading her missal and the little
booklets full of prayers and devotions in large print that Father
left on his visits, and waited for her children to come home.
She was never impatient: her imagination was too limited to
allow her to believe they were any place but at Church or on
the way to or from it, and her physical energies too low for her
to challenge her belief by a search for evidence to the contrary.
If she ever suspected the boys were not with them she never
betrayed the fact, and the girls would not hurt her by telling
her. In some ill-defined way she felt her weight to be an inter-
cessory agent between her children and a compassionate God
who must know how much of a barrier it was to her proper
practice of the Faith, and to theirs as well. She felt that if she
were not informed of their truancy (should there be any) neither
would God be, whose attention, she knew, was concentrated on
her at home. Often her rosary slipped to the floor from between her fat, sausagelike fingers, but her prayers went on
nevertheless, an endless, countless repetition of Our Fathers
and Hail Marys, unlimited because the finite number of beads
was no longer there to stop her.

Until she was twelve Ellen had never thought of herself as
an entity separate from her family. She was always "one of my
girls," or "one of the children," or, more enveloping, "Mrs.
Acton's youngest." Everywhere she went—and she could not remember going farther away than the Parish Hall, the grocery
store, school or occasionally to a neighborhood cut-rate store for
shoes or dress yard goods—she went with her family, and she
had never been in her mother's house alone. But one August
Saturday afternoon—the heat, the sickly smell of citronella and
the other sour smells of stale food still clung to her memory of
that day—her mother fainted as she sat on the love seat cutting
lengths of material for one of her gargantuan skirts. Ellen knew

their old Victorian house, which stood like an old soldier in a dingy line of identical New York brownstones. Even this constricted life narrowed when it was no longer possible for her mother to be moved at night—in an agonizing series of pushes and pulls, hoists and balanced restraints—up the steep stairs to her bedroom. So the dining room on the main floor became the heart of the family's life. Here Mrs. Acton slept on two day beds pushed together at one end of the long room. She ate sitting up on the bed, two bolsters stuffed behind her and the heavy oak dining-room table moved over before each meal for her massy arms to rest on. Her only move was to the love seat; here she said her unremitting rosaries, was dressed and undressed by her daughters, kissed dutifully by her sons when they left in the morning to be gone until long after she was put to bed at night. The house, once airy and capacious, had now become reduced to the dining room, shrunk to the dimensions of a single, unmoving body and the dim memory of its unlucky, deceased painter.

In high school Ellen did nothing but go to classes. At three she would walk home rapidly, bathed in an engulfing dread. Her terror by now was timeless: she could not remember when she had not been in its grip. She feared she would get home too late, that deep in that warm mountain of flesh the little spark of life that was her mother would flicker and go out, and that she would be sitting there, when she finally got home, overflowing the love seat, erect and dead. A kindly nun, spotting Ellen's ability to write good, clear compositions, offered her a staff position on the school newspaper, but it meant spending two full afternoons of editorial work at school each week. Her sisters were now working full time, and Ellen knew her mother would not object to being alone two more hours: her patience and willingness to wait were incomprehensible to her daughter. It was Ellen herself for whom the suspense of a longer day away from her mother was too great. She had to *know* that her mother was alive. She told Sister she needed the time for homework— and went home promptly at three.

By the time Ellen was graduated from Cathedral High her brothers had become merely pictures on the mantel across the room from her mother's love seat. One went into the Army and was sent to serve in Panama. Another became a salesman of hardware and brushes with a route in the South, and Billy, the youngest, married and moved to Rhode Island where his wife's family owned an undertaking parlor. They came home rarely and then only for a few hours, their eyes shifting quickly away from their mountainous mother whose voice, high and loving, seemed now to be expelled like a whistle from an insufficient mouth. Her conversations with them were limited to the only subject which had ever had any reality for her. She questioned them closely about their religious practices. With their eyes and their words they evaded her, in a fainthearted effort not to hurt her.

But at the end they came less and less often. Billy married a Presbyterian girl in a ceremony in her church in Providence, but this he could not bring himself to tell his mother. Regularly, on the birthday of Billy's daughter, at Christmas, and on the anniversaries of his baptism and his confirmation his mother sent holy cards, enfolding a number of medals or scapulars which Father O'Gara had blessed for her. Billy intercepted her letters and without opening them disposed of them before Dolores came down to breakfast. . . . A small allotment arrived each month from Private First Class Elliot Acton, Jr., but his mother never knew that the United States Army granted frequent furloughs to its soldiers: she regarded Army service as a full-time, unrelenting duty without letup of any sort . . . *And John, God bless him, so far away in Savannah, and the fare so terrible high.* Mrs. Acton prayed daily, constantly for them all, *all good boys, Father,* remembering them as they stood, erect and proud in their First Holy Communion suits. . . .

Ellen's sisters stayed home longer, sharing with Ellen the ritual care of their mother and the decaying house. Then, as if all at once they had realized that separately they would be powerless to effect a break, they all found it necessary to leave at once. This time, however, much more was said. The boys had gone away silently, fearing the inevitable guilt imposed upon them during explanations. Exactly as they had stopped going to Mass and novenas they stopped living at home. But the girls, who had never questioned the routine of arising at five-thirty every morning in winter and walking six blocks through icy New York streets to St. James, could not now leave the dining room that was their home without profuse and logical excuses. Mary, the oldest, married a boy she had never liked because he promised they would live on Long Island. Theresa, whose uncertain progress in high school discouraged her from continuing beyond the second year, became a practical nurse after some study reluctantly financed by John at his mother's request. Offered a number of jobs upon completion of her training, she took one in Syracuse, New York. She sat on a footstool beside the love seat fingering the old black-beaded rosary she had found on the floor at her mother's feet, and explained that this position with a wealthy family—a fine *Catholic* family with five young children —offered the best pay. What she did not explain, in her profuse, easy flow of guilt-propelled words was that it was the only position offered to her outside the New York area.

Now Ellen and Martha were alone with the elephantine, aging woman. Circling around her, impelled toward her by a force in no way diminished by the degrading acts they had to perform for her—she was now too large to make the numerous trips to the bathroom that her weakened bladder demanded—Martha was finally driven by love and pity, and a deep, genuine piety, to join an Order, the Sisters of Mercy who had taught the Acton children for so long. Ellen, motivated by her old fear, and nurturing a growing and ashamed hatred of the object of her servitude, was left alone, endlessly (it seemed to her) to share her mother's dining-room existence.

Except by the very grossness of her being, Mrs. Acton gave Ellen no reason for hatred, and this made it harder for Ellen to bear her feeling. Her mother's pride was divided without favoritism among her absent children, although Martha, now Sister Mary Martha Avicenna, whose visit was a monument in her mother's year, was a name most often invoked when she spoke to her few clerical and religious callers. But she made no demands upon Ellen and was openly, freely grateful for everything she did for her. Her greatest concern was for her meals, but even here Ellen grew ashamed of the ease with which she could be served. The amount of food she had consumed in her life was so great that by its very bulk it had dulled her senses, and she no longer knew the precise difference between one kind and another. Or perhaps it was that her uncommon haste to consume the enormous portions set before her precluded any time for discrimination. Four or five pounds of any one food would satisfy her for a few hours, and even the same food in the same proportions repeated at the next meal. But often she could not wait once the time came to be fed, and her beads would slip between her trembling fingers to the floor, her lips would be incapable of prayer, her sparse, still-black hair would become wet with the eagerness of her avidity, and all her immensity was then concentrated on her great need to eat.

Because Ellen could not bear to contemplate, even through the screen of her secret hatred, what she conceived to be her mother's lonely, mindless existence during the long days she was at school (the same kindly nun had pushed her firmly into Hunter College, aided by very high verbal scores on her College Boards and a State Regents scholarship), Ellen would do her preparations aloud at night in the dining room. Her mother understood very little of what she said—Child Psychology, Melville and Whitman, Philosophy of Religion—but she was reassured by the sound of the growingly confident young voice. She was not alone, and she sat attentively, her ear catching the tones of Ellen's voice reading, her own lips constantly forming the words of the Memorare and the Hail Mary, her head a tragic, small melon atop the mound of formless human flesh, a living, bloated reproach to Ellen's normalcy.

And just as she performed, undeviatingly, the ritual of her mother's care, like some aboriginal dance, she went on with all the demanding practices of her religious life. Like a marionette, her inner life was composed only of the outer strings of motion. She made her progress from one ceremony to another, following the old, absolute pattern, and only after she had, almost by accident, gravitated into Professor Gwyn Llewellyn's class in Philosophy of Religion did she realize that his scorn and logic were cutting at the strings and that she was in danger of coming apart spiritually.

Now in the evenings in the dining room Ellen worked silently, dogged by self-doubts, and her mother, equally pleased by everything Ellen did, went on smiling over her prayers. Ellen read Whitehead and Russell, Morris Raphael Cohen and Sidney Hook for Professor Llewellyn's course and struggled with the thought that her whole existence thus far had been a solidified and formalized gymnastic. She realized that in a curious way her religion and her mother were the same thing. To both she paid the same unmindful attentions. She worshipped in the same way as she cared for her mother, it was now clear to her, with her legs and feet, her muscles, tendons and shoulder blades. By virtue of Mrs. Acton's tragic physical presence and the fear of death which she symbolized for Ellen, her mother had maintained her in an unquestioning inertia, during which she genuflected, crossed herself and pounded her breast in *mea culpas*. But now the words echoing out of her childhood evenings on her knees, the catechetical instructions to which she was still able to return word-perfect lip service, the numerous prayers and litanies recited from memory at the proper moment during the Mass, the Creed, were all suddenly suspect, shells in which the vital organisms had long since died. The dogma she knew by heart, so well that her very absolute possession of the words, which had once seemed to be evidence of their truth, now appeared to her to be as dead and decayed as the remains of Miss Haversham's wedding feast.

Ellen never gave her mother any indication of this cataclysm in her thoughts. But because she was, by now at twenty-two, a woman of deeply grained habits to whom it seemed as if life

would have no form if it were to lose its regularity, she carried
the black night of her soul to Father Morley. He had grown
old and sick, and was pastor of St. James in name only. His
two energetic assistants drove about the parish making visits and
performing all his functions while he sat in the rectory, composed
and good-humored, but resentful of his uselessness to his people.

He received Ellen rather gruffly. He knew she would not have
come if her trouble had been simple, and he felt too ill to be
very patient with the ephemeral trials of a mind in a healthy
body. But he had always been fond of her—of her family would
perhaps be closer to it, thought Ellen as she watched him struggle for politeness when she asked if she might talk to him—
and he allowed her to talk at once of her difficulties. When she
had finished telling him of her discoveries about herself, and
of her belief that she was losing her faith, Father Morley
coughed deeply, spread his entwined fingers over his chest for
a few moments (Ellen was to learn later that a cancer was
growing in his esophagus), and then told her that only now, in
the midst of her blackest doubts, was she in danger of becoming a true Catholic.

"How can that be?"

"Because, my young friend, you've lived all your life without
once considering what all the walking to and fro and kneeling
and breast-beating are about. But now suddenly you realize this,
and so you think they must be about nothing."

"But the philosophers I've been reading believe that all re-
ligions are nothing but these conventions followed blindly, and
that Catholicism is one of the worst. It's complex and ritual-
istic, and its liturgy is meaningless tradition based on human
fear and superstition."

"And do you?"

"What?"

"Believe all that?"

"I don't really know what I believe at this point."

"Good. You've advanced from your overly prolonged child-

hood of not really knowing what you believe but behaving as
if you did. If it will make you feel any truer to yourself and
to your professor (is he a professor of *religion*, did you say?) it
might be a good idea to behave for a while as if you didn't
believe, and see what you have left. Stop all the lip service and
ritualism, as you call it and as you seem to feel it is for you,
and stand apart for a bit. See what's left. You can't wish God
into your life, although He's there sure as death whether you
give Him *lebensraum* or not, but once you see Him there, no
amount of high philosophizing or symbolic logic or semantics
and whatever else it is they teach you up there will rid you of
Him."

"The Hound of Heaven, eh?"

"Yes, and a monkey on your back and the stone of Sisyphus
and the Procrustean bed and even, a voracious fist of cells in
your chest," and he touched his own again.

Then he breathed deeply and went on: "Those big men,
thinkers, logicians that you talk about. I haven't read 'em, probably now never will, but I've been under the impression that
the difference between them and us is that they put up a bigger
and much better fight against belief than we could ever do.
They've all the proper scholarly apparatus and all the vocabu-
lary, and some of them will go on tying Him down with strings
like Gulliver as long as they live. But He won't be reasoned
away any more easily than He can be reasoned *into* their belief."

"Isn't this rather unorthodox advice? I mean, to stay away
from the sacraments . . ."

"You'll not be gone long, my friend," said Father Morley,
smiling and tired. "You'll be back, hungry, at the rail, because
the emptiness without Him will appall you. You can't live on
air like a chameleon if you're a pelican who's tasted its own
blood."

"Where'd you come upon all the bestiary stuff?" asked Ellen,
still young enough to be surprised by learning in anyone except a student or a member of a college faculty.

"Oh, I've got very lit'ry now that I'm no use as a man of

action. You see, I'm really very safe giving this advice. These last months I've been standing back too, looking at what was left after all the dust of my forty years of perpetual motion had settled. And I know what I found there. Far more than I would have believed after all this time. Christ himself, in all his loneliness and despair and goodness, Christ away from the polychrome holy cards and down from the painted plaster models, all passion spent . . . He, *Himself*, without words or symbols for Him, sitting in that pit of me, that black private cell in the center of my being that your professors like to call psyche or personality but which I call soul . . . which, is, after all, as good a place as any to entertain Him."

Father Morley was now visibly exhausted. Ellen got up to go. "Thank you, Father. I'll try. . . ."

"One last word, Ellen Acton my girl. Don't stay away too long, contemplating yourself. The sacraments aren't the whole of it, but they're the rope ladder to the rescue ship and the lifeline to the Rescuer. You won't get back without them."

"I'll try, Father. And take care of yourself."

"I don't need to. I'm already provided for, I suspect."

On the floor of the Faculty Room, her blind, open eyes fixed on the empty pad on her lap, Ellen breathed deeply, remembering it all. A year after her visit Father Morley had died. And because events of this kind come in a chain linked to each other by a mystical, communicable failure of energy, her mother had died soon after. As she slept one night her heart had stopped beating. When Ellen came in the morning to begin the long job of raising her to a sitting position, she could not be moved. The fluid, viscous flesh had cooled and hardened. Ellen's great fear, her beast in the jungle, was laid to rest with her mother. Ellen saw her mother's life as doomed to ludicrous failure by a tragic imbalance of glands and blood chemistry. Only her death in an appropriate position rescued her from terminating in farce as Ellen had so feared. Little by little, teaching, a professional

interest in her students and the graduate work she did as she
worked at teaching jobs filled the void left by the departure of
the only real fidelity and the only genuine hatred she had ever
known.

Ellen's silent and successfully buried emotion for her mother
never died. Although she was free of her at twenty-eight, the
enervating hatred turned inward upon itself, filling the spaces
within her with wariness, with mistrust of other human beings
who might look to her for help. She felt her long bondage had
marked her as one of life's natural servants, and that it would
never again be possible for her to form a relationship of any
other kind. Reluctant to stand emotionally close enough to anyone to be caught and held, Ellen's loneliness was marked, and
interpreted by those who lived with her variously, as scorn, or
self-sufficiency, or as the reserve of a born solitary. No one saw
her clearly for what she was—a woman who feared dependence
of others upon her and who quickly turned away from any
claimant upon her assistance.

Her years at Miss Hands coincided roughly with her return
to the Church. Since she lived so much alone within teaching
communities her return went unnoticed. Father Morley, who
would have cared, had been dead for some time. Had he not
been, Ellen would still not have expected any notice to be taken
of what for her was an epic journey home; like an elderly relative whom one fails to notify of a long-delayed arrival, it was
not to be expected that anyone would be at the depot to meet
the train. She joined no parish group, and refused an invitation
to address a meeting of the Rosary Altar Society ("on *anything* about education, or teaching, or that sort of thing," the
president had written her). Slowly she forced her way back into
the practices of her childhood, which only recently had seemed
to her as distant as catacomb Christianity.

But even while she knew she believed and was convinced of
what intellectually she had always understood, she often still
questioned the basis in practice of her returned belief. Dogma

no longer troubled her but rather the dichotomy for her between faith and action. Now in her maturity—she was now close to forty although she had held aging off rather well and her composed, well-matched features had taken no unpleasant turns and lost none of the tautness of youth—she saw her personal faith as infected by a suicidal separatism, a deadly gulf that existed for her between Christianity and being a Christian. Her acceptance of the doctrine of suffering and pain was academic, since she found it impossible any longer to come close to it in its human manifestation. Even her acquaintance with the pain of love was literary. Like her mother she had relegated men who sought her out—there had been a few in her early thirties—to the negative, and to the past tense. She said of one: "He was rather dull, but then, I never knew him well," although neither of these judgments was true of Henry Lasky or William Moore or the others. Ellen said these things to excuse her rejection of their approaches, and buried them in the past, as her mother had buried Elliot Acton, Sr., among their faults and her unapproachable reserve.

The crucifix was true and real, the Figure on it caught historically in a moment of everlasting pain, but because she could not bear immediacy, it was always for Ellen a symbol of the unreachable past. What she knew, after the distance of years and the loosening of the cords of daily involvement, to be her mother's encased martyrdom, still had the power to make her feel nothing but abhorrence, to make her resolve against permitting herself proximity ever again to any human catastrophe.

Nothing important was permitted to touch Ellen now. The minor annoyances of school life, her irritation at the Headmistress's incompetence (most Headmistresses were incompetent, she had concluded, and only inertia and sentimentality retained them in their places), her impatience at the stupidity of students and faculty, intruded upon her privacy but never reached the dark pit that Father Morley had located in himself and surveyed so well within her.

Trudy Langer, Ruthie Vandermeer and Nan Kittredge lounged against the steps of Elias Cook Hall. In the blaze of noon sun the girls resembled castaways without the energy, after a struggle to attain the beach, to take shelter anywhere.

"Trudy, you *are* planning to return that key to her room, aren't you?"

"I suppose, sooner or later."

"There'll be hell to pay if she finds it's gone." Ruthie wanted no enemies, especially those in a position to affect her final mark. Although Miss Seward did not teach her she shared the generally held superstition that the faculty consulted with each other when they wrote comments and grades so that there would be no discrepancy, no sudden contradictions about talents or achievement.

"Hell, she'll never know. You know, I just remembered something about Eleanor Ames. When she was here wasn't she the girl who printed the picture in *The Writing Hand* of girls toasting each other at a pajama party with cans of ale? Wasn't she photography editor when we were freshmen?"

"I think so. She was an early scurvy elephant, a prophet."

There was a short, exhausted silence.

"There goes Miss Parks going into Arts."

"Yup. The council gathers. Watch for the smoke. It will rise when decision is made. They burn the white papers. Let's have a smoke ourselves. After all, we shouldn't waste the key."

"And then you'll return it?" Ruthie persisted.

"For Godsakes. Oh sure. Me. And who will bell the cat?"

"Well, you took it. And I'd like to see if I have any mail."

"Meet you."

"Yup."

Madame Mifflin met Mademoiselle Loivin who had not been expected to attend Chapel because she was busy packing for her return to Paris. Together they walked toward the Buttery.

"How I envy you, to be going back!" said Madame.

"I'm glad too. But I shall miss you all." The little French girl, because of her extreme courtesy and shyness, had only seen the surface of her house mates; and the Americans, in an effort to make some sort of pleasant national impression, had shown her only the agreeable social side of themselves.

She went on, overcome by her feelings of kindliness even toward Madame who had been most caustic and critical of her accent: "I should be glad to get in touch with your daughter and son while I am in Switzerland vacationing. If you would please give me their addresses."

The charity in these words was in direct proportion to the overwhelming gratitude that the young Frenchwoman felt at being allowed to go home, as well as her pleasure at the attempts at friendliness of the other teachers. For in truth she had spent long hours listening politely to Madame's tales of her children. Indeed she had found it impossible to avoid them, but her innate courtesy was so great that she listened without protest, and often appeared to be eager for anecdotes, like a child pestering her nurse for more stories with the same hero and heroine.

"I am not entirely sure where they are at this moment, they move around a great deal, you know. Jean is with the diplomatic . . . and Dorothea on the staff, the art staff of *Réalités*, and so she travels to the shows. But when I find out I will let you know, if you will give me your mailing address in Paris. . . ."

"I will. Are you now going to lunch?"

"Oh yes, and do you know, I have just had a most interesting talk with the Junior English Mistress. She has told me, you will be interested in this . . ."

Meg Miers put her brushes in the sink, shook her head sorrowfully at a portrait of a young Negro boy she'd been working on for some weeks, from memory, and left the Studio. She was hungry, and self-criticism was always most acute at such times. *Someday I'll cut away from all this, and really paint, not just in between times and after I've cleaned up the kids' mess, but only paint, just paint. Maybe.* Her resolution gave way before her hunger and she started across the grass to the Buttery.

Sophie reached into her pocket to lock the stage door after her long and futile attempt at repairing the curtain. There was no key there. Then she remembered she had come in through the auditorium. She considered briefly where she might have left the key, found she could not possibly remember, latched the door from the inside and went out the auditorium door. She wasn't hungry. All the defeats and humiliations of the day sat like a great tumor at the bottom of her throat, and she knew she would not be able to swallow anything. She walked down the hall to her classroom and, seated at her desk took out her pad and began her quarterly struggle with the truth: "Patricia is a girl whose good intentions and hard efforts will perhaps . . ."

Ellen's notebook for May— 196—:

The Twins seem on the outs and hardly talk to each other. On occasion, almost in the rhythm of manic-depressives, all their mingled sexual rancors rise up and confront each other and they fight terribly—you can hear them all over the House. The rest of us cringe in our cells, thinking this must be some kind of supranatural war, above and beyond us, like the ancient one between God and Lucifer. Then, because their need for each other seems greater than their need of peace, they subside and are almost silently reconciled. . . . Reminds me of Macbeth calling out: "Put rancors in the vessel of my peace."

At Cape Canaveral they say "it is scrubbed" meaning stopped, not going through as planned. Is the origin of this the old-fashioned blackboard which still is used for schedules in some industries—the theatre too I think—just as "cancelled" might have its origin in the act of crossing out by pencil? American optimism. AOK to the astronaut means perfect. Less than perfect has thus far not been used in print.

An old textbook left on my shelves by my predecessor contains an essay by a nineteenth-century physiologist who begins his description of his early studies in organisms with this: "I soon learned, however, that to seem to be still is not to be dead, and that to move is not always to be alive."

Writing, I find, is an antihuman, almost suicidal, occupation. Like the spider who was thought in the Middle Ages to weave his web out of fibers unwound from his own breast (Fr. M. would have liked this), the writer uses himself constantly until his sustenance is pulled out of him and he is left, a shell, a hand-puppet.

Henry Fielding has Mrs. Slipslop talk suspiciously like her mistress and yet her class shines through the elegant phrases. In another sense I see this happening here. I talk in class of the symbols of the Fat Lady and the Chicken Sandwiches in Salinger and later in the hall I hear someone shout, "Come on, Fat Lady, we've got studying to do." And it works the other way too: I've twice found myself thinking of Liz Rankin as a scurvy elephant.

Last night at the faculty music hour: there are two types of listeners to music, those who are propelled at once by the music into their own dreams—any music, but always I think, into the same dreams—and those in whom music produces an unusual and delightful state of euphoria. For its duration these second types are strangely happy, they seem to love those seated near them, and they smile uninterruptedly at those across the room. Any music will produce this state in them. . . . And for me music is nothing but connective tissue to words. Once I have climbed out along it, as on a ledge, and jumped, I am in

the solid world of sentences, and naturally I cannot climb back.
. . . The true listener, I suspect, does none of these things
but is suspended in a kind of natural, visceral element parallel
to that of the music itself and directly related to it *at every
point*, and, like outer space, without the possibility of escape
until the last note has been played.

I have decided that administering a delicate operation like
this school is an impossible task. The Headmistress must please
the Board of Governors, the parents, the alumnae, the students
and the faculty—in that order. "I come, Graymalkin!"

Yet Malraux claims that "all art is a means to gain hold on
fate," so writing cannot be entirely suicidal. Although I would
have thought it was more clearly a means of escaping fate. "Art
lives by reason of its function, which is to enable men to break
free from their human condition." Gallant. Impossible.

Re: uniforms. The girls seem constantly to rebel against wearing them. At a class meeting today Trudy L. said wearing them
converts them all to "hideous conformists," psychologically. My
sympathy for her view was dissipated later in the day when I
watched the students leave the campus for their free, in-town
afternoon. Everyone of them in a tan raincoat, flat brown loafers, fuzzy ankle socks, a pair of pigskin (I think) gloves. And
underneath, all of them being hideous individualists by not
wearing any part of their uniforms.

Oddly, Liz Rankin plays the piano rather well, although she
attacks it as if she hated everyone within earshot.

CHAPTER IV

Office of the Headmistress

THE Disciplinary Committee met in Miss Blount's office. She had shut the door, a conspicuous exception to her rule. Miss Blount proclaimed often that she wanted the students and the faculty to feel no separation between her function and their needs. Ellen, by virtue of longevity the senior member of the committee, placed an uncharitable interpretation upon the Headmistress's open-door policy: it seemed another symptom of her everlasting curiosity. Having little grasp of current educational theory, and being vague about the pragmatic details of high school curriculum, she filled her working days with the minutiae of the girls' behavior, rejoiced at minor infractions of the rules, little signs of aberration in deportment, because they afforded her an opportunity for her brand of compassionate action. Through her open door she could watch the faculty move through the hall, note the formation of any new alliance, eavesdrop upon sudden spates of furious words. From it too she had a clear view across the seedy court into Miss Rankin's office and could prepare herself beforehand for crises that had first been brought to her assistant.

Closing the door now upon the little bunches of students going to and from music lessons (she remembered Mr. James had been in this morning which must account for all the feverish racing back and forth to the practice rooms of students carrying dog-eared copies of *The Moonlight Sonata* and the Bach *Inventions*), was an act designed to raise the tone of this meeting to the level of conspiracy, a cabal of the Upper People on a high professional level. While Ellen, Jo and Elizabeth Rankin watched her the Headmistress bent over at her curious angle to adjust the blinds on her enormous picture window. Due to some myopia on the part of the architect and to the determined forty-five degree angle in which it nestled, the Headmistress's office looked directly, disconcertingly, into the picture window of the library, the two rooms forming the angle of one side of the building's hollow triangle. Full afternoon sun flooded the room. The teachers looked down at the table at once to avoid the cruel glare. Miss Blount's energy—now she was rearranging the chairs around the two coffee tables of uneven height which served as her conference table—was limitless, discouraging. The faculty waited wearily for her to sit down.

"Are we to deal today with that foolishness last night *and* Miss Seward's accusation, or may I raise a recent and more pressing issue?" asked Miss Rankin. Her face glowed with the joy of her role as accuser-with-evidence, and her voice cut through Miss Blount's dilatory, housekeeping motions: now the Headmistress set out scratch pads and well-sharpened yellow pencils before each teacher, and rearranged the pattern of her strays of hair, while frowning down at the small sheet of notes before her. Miss Blount hated disciplinary committee meetings; Miss Rankin loved them and so she focused all her energies on pinning down Miss Blount's vague dismissals of issues, and her obscuring of real points by pleasantries, irrelevancies and physical dartings here and there.

The Headmistress was startled. "Do you mean the play?"

"No. I mean the way Miss Seward claims the seniors used the play to ridicule her." Miss Rankin's intent was to be coldly reportorial but each word was ringed with scorn.

"But Miss Rankin, I don't see how that can be a matter for this committee. After all . . ."

Ellen had had enough of this jockeying for fence position. "Miss Rankin means that if we consider Sophie's accusations that Trudy Langer cheated while she was proctoring the *Hamlet* quiz, Trudy's behavior last night may then throw light on the whole matter."

"I think that makes sense," said Jo, who was willing to do anything to hurry the meeting along. She was already feeling impatient; she had only agreed to sit on this committee this year to avoid another more active assignment like props for plays or business adviser of *The Writing Hand*. The end of the year always found her short of interest in these little disciplinary skirmishes and longing to be off to the major engagement of her life, at the Cape.

Now the Headmistress was confused. She retreated to a maneuver she had often used before. Looking down at her printed pad which said: THINGS TO DO TODAY; IN THIS ORDER, she read: "Miss Seward declared on May"—she had forgotten to note the date but she went on bravely—"declared one day last week that Gertrude Langer, a senior student, had with her in her jacket pocket at a quiz in the Senior English Room a paper containing the whole of 'Oh what a rogue and peasant slave am I? written in tiny, almost microscopic printing. Miss Seward further claims she copied from this paper to answer a question on the test requiring a soliloquy from *Hamlet* that one had memorized to be written out."

Miss Blount hesitated. She was finding it hard to read her notes. Holding the sheet a little closer to her face she read on:

"Trudy Langer, on being confronted with this report by me on the following day, denied it, saying paper she handled was a piece of scrap paper on which she had *practiced* writing the soliloquy before putting it finally into her blue book."

The Headmistress looked slowly from one member of the committee to another, as if to allow the entire justice of the denial to sink in, and to take full effect. Complete anarchy had now taken over the arrangement of her hair, intensifying the deep vertical ruts in her cheeks and giving to her face an unusual severity. Then she moved easily into the second stage of her maneuver:

"Miss Rankin, as executive secretary of this committee, perhaps you would like to regulate the discussion. I prefer to listen and then to judge the case—with of course the assistance of all of you."

The tightening of Miss Rankin's lips were the only indication she gave of her surprise at the newly bestowed title of "executive" secretary. No one could have guessed at the pleasure that filled her at the sound of the word. And, like a soldier who receives a battlefield promotion, she moved at once to take command. She passed her notebook and poised pencil, which she had prepared for use in her minutes-taking secretarial capacity, to Ellen who scowled but picked up the pencil. She then straightened the blank paper in front of her so that it was perfectly aligned with the edge of the table and placed a pencil at a perfect angle to the top of the paper. She had secured her command post, settled in, and was ready to begin.

"Shall we assume that Trudy's explanation is a possible, indeed an entirely reasonable one?" she asked flatly.

"Hold on now," said Jo, her sense of justice offended by the new chairman's highhandedness. "How can you assume that, knowing her?"

For a long moment each of them dealt with her private knowledge of Trudy Langer.

Ellen: *Trudy Langer is an unhappy, sullen and often dishonest girl. But we can assume that, because that is the safe and compassionate way for the Headmistress to handle a dishonest student of influential parents.*

Elizabeth Rankin: *We will assume that because clearly it implies the utter incompetence of Sophie Seward who was hired by Arvilla Blount, Headmistress.*

Jo: *We can assume that because it will get this damn thing over sooner, and I can get out of here and back to all the correcting and Comments I've left for this deceptively free Saturday.*

Miss Blount said: "It seems a reasonable assumption," and

thought: *we* must *assume it because to discover anything else would cost us a great deal more than I can tell them and gain us nothing except a small piece of gratification for a woman who, after all, is soon to be leaving here.*

In the hot room no one spoke for a few moments. Ellen wished the door could be opened. Jo looked longingly at the open blinds, wishing she had the courage, in the face of the Headmistress's deep dislike of using the electric lights, to get up and shut them. But, like prisoners at a lengthy third degree, they felt powerless to do anything about the oppressive heat of the room.

Jo asked: "When did Sophie find the crib paper? I confess I've only heard vague rumors about this whole business but nothing definite."

Rapidly the Headmistress read her notes. Obviously she could find no notation on this aspect of the matter. "It doesn't say. Why do you think that is important?"

"Well, if Sophie says she had the crib sheet early in the exam, at the very beginning as a matter of fact, then clearly it *was* a crib sheet. But if she found it halfway through the exam or near the end, then Sophie has no case at all."

"Did you ask Miss Seward when she found it?" asked Miss Rankin quietly, knowing the answer and so giving to her question a deceptively offhand tone.

"I did not. I considered the intent important, not a small detail like that. And I've known Trudy well for four years. I've never had any evidence that she would do a thing like this, nor has any other *long-time* member of this faculty, and I refuse to believe it on the evidence, which might well be mistaken or at the least biased, of one new and . . . and often . . . upset member of the faculty."

The three teachers stared at the marred surface of the coffee table during the Headmistress's fevered recital of her feelings on the matter.

Miss Rankin was not, however, to be moved out of her newly won judicial position by this display of heat. "I see," she said. "But perhaps, to satisfy the others on the Committee who don't know her as well, Miss Blount, we might call in Miss Seward and settle this one point?"

Oh Lord, this is going to take forever, finding her and bringing her here, thought Jo. She said, "I suggest we adjourn, having the *executive* secretary ask Miss Seward about it at her convenience, and report back to us at another meeting on Monday."

Miss Rankin was not going to allow her new authority to end so quickly. "Miss Blount, I submit that this would be too late. I will be working on final reports and grades this week end, the diplomas are being printed, and if any action is to be taken it has to be taken today. Furthermore, there is no room in the schedule for another meeting on Monday or *any* day next week."

The specter of the Schedule is being lowered, thought Ellen, like a *deus ex machina,* to settle matters finally.

The very thought of action sent the Headmistress into a panic. Her most successful tactic during her years in office was the avoidance of taking action of any kind, of promising a later decision and then allowing time itself to bury it under a mound of human forgetfulness and the natural decline all urgent matters suffer. She would give the matter, she would say confidently, to a committee for consideration, and then neglect to appoint the committee or, if pressed, appoint to it faculty members whose opinion on the matter under consideration was known to her to be safe and conservative. Or, more lethal than all other procedures, she would promise to bring the question before the Board of Governors who, she well knew, would not meet again before the issue had entirely lost its urgency. In this way she believed she had avoided a good deal of unpleasantness and certainly some radical moves which she would have regretted later.

"*Whenever* the paper was found, it seems to me, would not affect the truth of Trudy's story. She might have started to write as soon as she sat down. Children often do that, to be sure they don't forget something they've just recently memorized." Miss Blount considered herself profoundly knowing in all the byways of the young psyche which she always called the "child-mind."

"But if she were found to have it *before* the exam was given out?" persisted Ellen, who sensed that the Headmistress was in danger of going off on one of her beloved discussions of child psychology and hoped somehow to head her off by clinging stubbornly to the point.

Miss Blount decided to abandon cold logic which she always found detrimental to her success in any argument. "*Whenever* she was found to have it does not affect her intent, which I say again has never been dishonest and could not have been so this time, this close to graduation and all."

Jo said, grinning: "All right. I don't know the girl very well. Had her just one year in American History, and I don't recall her saying very much except: 'I don't know' and 'I'm not prepared.' And I'll admit those were both *very* honest statements. But if you say you know her to be incapable of this sort of thing I'll go along with you. Anything else on the agenda?"

"I agree," said Miss Rankin promptly, anxious to move on to her private grievance.

Ellen sat back, huddled within herself. Her customary posture at meetings was to say nothing, to go along with the Headmistress's easy permissiveness, with Elizabeth Rankin's obscure conniving, with Jo's eagerness to be gone . . . Yet there *was* a point, and it lay deeper, goading a strangely new sense of responsibility that she had rarely before felt. "I have loved justice and hated iniquity . . ." St. Gregory, the Seventh, Pope and confessor, buried for centuries in the Mass for today, his gallant, lonely struggle resuscitated once a year in the missals of a few old women and men, frightened young virgins and boys-to-be priests who happened into Church on this hot May weekday, quoting the psalmist as he died. . . . And I?

"It does matter, does it not, that she realize she was wrong in what she did, if we know for certain of course that she was?

So there is a point in finding out how just Miss Seward's accusation is. If we don't, we might well be jeopardizing Trudy's whole future." Ellen heard herself saying words almost before they were formulated in her mind. She had time before her question to feel surprised at the sound of her own voice. "Don't you think so, Miss Blount?"

Miss Blount sensed danger. "I think, Miss Acton, that it is really important to know whether, in her nervous and uncertain way, Miss Seward is making another of her mistakes. But not at the cost of publicly questioning one of our senior students. Even if Trudy did this, I don't see the earth-shaking importance of it. Everyone makes mistakes. Are we to pillory our girls, who after all are growing, changing little organisms, for one misstep? And just before their graduation, when we may well suppose they are under abnormal stress anyway?"

Ellen for so long had lived in the neutral zone where she permitted herself no involvement in the affairs of others that now she felt unprepared for the fray. Her moral armor was rusty, but she decided to try one final lance.

"The importance of it is not to us but to her, I think. To succeed once—and her success will be the greater for her because she must know Sophie reported this to us, and she will conclude we decided, for whatever reason, to take no action—is to encourage her in other efforts like this. It is precisely because we *are* graduating her that we owe her some action, some direction. . . ."

"But Miss Acton . . ." the Headmistress was beside herself in her anxiety to blanket, in whatever way she could, this dangerous blaze, "It's not as if it were a final . . . or . . . or a big unit test or something like that. It was only a little quiz."

Elizabeth Rankin stared at the Headmistress. She had sat silent through the gradual weakening of the Headmistress's position, watching her grant at one moment what she had only the moment before categorically denied, watching her back up rapidly while pretending slowly to advance, like a bravado schoolboy challenging the town bully before an audience of his fellows. Now she grew red and taut at the Headmistress's final tactical error. Fixedly she stared at the blank agenda paper.

Jo too looked at Miss Blount unbelievingly; she said nothing.

Ellen's long training in withdrawal suddenly deserted her. For the first time since she had turned her anger against her deserting brothers and sisters, against her omnipresent mother, and then vowed to disengage herself from all causes forever, she felt fury rising in her, a choking, blinding, unreasoning fury at her own cowardice in the face of the flagrant moral gray that confronted her. *One cannot coexist with it.* For the first time in all the years of her emotional exile she tasted the flavor of righteous combat even while knowing that the cause was doomed to failure. In a voice louder and clearer than she thought she could command, she said:

"To say she has only cheated on a little quiz, Miss Blount, is rather like claiming that one is only a little pregnant!"

The sun, in one last notable burst of energy, moved over beyond the rim of the picture window, and the room was silent, without its glare, much darker than it had been a moment before.

"Shall we get on," said Miss Rankin, after a pause, making a declarative sentence out of the grammatical question. She appeared to be making a mental note, inwardly resolving on some course of action. Ellen felt weary as she watched her work the fine point of her pencil viciously into the blank sheet before her, the deep tiredness of the platoon leader who returns to report defeat of his gallant attempt. Outnumbered, pinned down by cross fire . . .

Jo had briefly entertained the delightful notion that, having freed Trudy of any immediate danger, they would, to mark the Headmistress's gratitude, all be dismissed.

"To what?" she asked.

"To the matter I mentioned before, and which has far greater immediacy than a minor case of cribbing which, granted it did happen, is, as we all very well know, one of the occupational hazards of our profession and without which," she added in a tone she felt to be whimsical, "there would be very little for us ever to talk about."

"What is this matter you keep hinting at?" asked Miss Blount who did not enjoy Miss Rankin's little joke at this time. To her, ever since her teaching days had stopped, the profession had taken on the air of a holy activity not to be spoken of lightly, especially by its priestesses.

"This morning just after breakfast I smelled smoke near the stage-door entrance to the auditorium. I sat for a while in my classroom from which I have an excellent view of that door. I saw three girls come out, locking the door behind them. Afterwards I went in through the auditorium and discovered three cigarette butts which had been put out on the wood-work at the bottom of the lighting panel and then dropped behind the black curtain."

Ellen felt a stirring of admiration for Miss Rankin. It was not only the care with which she had pursued each aspect of the misdemeanor that made her marvel, but the restraint, the carefully planned delaying tactic that had enabled her not to dash out and accost the girls immediately but instead to wait, to hover, savoring the future revelation, sacrificing the satisfactions of the moment for the still greater ones of the future.

"Damn lucky they didn't burn the place down," said Jo.

Miss Blount paled visibly. "Who was it?"

"Nancy Kittredge, Ruth Vandermeer and Gertrude Langer."

"Oh fine," said Ellen under her breath. "Trudy, the soul of honor." .

Miss Blount, filled with horror at the thought of the costly catastrophe that had so narrowly been averted, was no longer listening to the teachers. "They locked the door behind them, did you say, Miss Rankin? Where would they get a key to that door?"

"That perplexed me too, Miss Blount. Do you have yours?"

"Yes. Oh yes. Here . . . I'm sure. Somewhere here." She

began a confused search through her desk drawers, hindered by the meager amount of light in the corner of the room. Triumphantly, miraculously, she held up a key.

Ellen groaned inwardly. She remembered she had lent hers to Sophie during rehearsals for the ill-fated *Merchant of Venice*. She braced herself.

"You have a key, haven't you, Ellen?" pursued Miss Rankin, like a hound who has just now picked up the scent.

"Yes."

"Do you have it with you?"

"No. Miss Seward's been using it during rehearsals."

"It must be that key they used," said the Headmistress, pleased at her ability to follow the discussion this far.

"Obviously," said Miss Rankin. "But how did the girls get it?"

"That," said Miss Blount grimly, "we shall find out."

Action, for so long a dreaded foe, a course to be avoided at all costs, had at this moment become a holy crusade.

"I thought you were meeting this afternoon," said Madame to Ellen who sat down beside her on a bench under Eighty-Eight Tree. A huge sugar maple whose trunk had been serrated with generations of carved initials, it was the gift of the class of 1888 and the Faculty House's sole source of shade.

"Carried over until four," replied Ellen wearily. She leaned her head back against the tree and closed her eyes.

"So? How did it go?" Madame's curiosity was always at its highest pitch about Disciplinary Committee meetings because by constitution they were secret and their proceedings confidential.

"Hot."

"Is not it so. Was Trudy's cheating discussed?"

"Who told you about that?"

"Oh, a student who felt it was only right all the faculty

should know, not just the Committee, and I think she was right."

Ruthie Vandermeer, thought Ellen, *pushing for that A in French.*

"As a matter of fact it was Ruthie Vandermeer. She told me of it, sitting as she did next to the girl."

"What else did she tell you?"

"She said Miss Seward shook so much she dropped the paper and then Trudy—can you believe this?—picked it up and gave it to her again with a smile. And she said, Ruthie that is, that she could not look at Miss Seward because there were tears on Miss Seward's face."

Ellen sat unmoving, her eyes still closed, hoping Madame would sense her tiredness and be still. But Madame was off, engrossed in a connection she had just thought of between Trudy's felony and a similar case that had once cropped up in Dorothea's Swiss *l'école des femmes.* Her mobile black eyes flashing with delighted reminiscence, she explored all the avenues of the anecdote, its complex and Freudian implications, and described the special light of heroism in which her daughter was bathed by her staunch adherence to the truth.

Ellen thought: *a man is not always alive when he moves. Something like that. I'm full of bits and snatches today, like Nanki-Poo, like a patch-quilt my mother once put together laboriously out of pieces of my father's old suits and her dresses and stained dresser scarves . . . little memories . . . that to seem to be still is not to be dead. . . .*

". . . but that little cannot last her long, is not it so, and I will never expect repayment, you can be sure. It is a gift, I told her so. . . ."

Madame's words on their ascendant French tones swept past Ellen. Half asleep under Eighty-Eight Tree in the exhausting heat and deep in her personal and literary tangle, she heard none of the transformed story of unbelievable stupidity and great charity.

Trudy Langer was alone in her room in Elias Cook. She had dropped her sweaty jeans on the floor and was now wearing a pair of faded plaid bermudas. Her roommate, after a few nasty words had passed between them, decided it would be best to go to the library to read, and had left Trudy in sole possession of her black mood. Indeed, Trudy had instigated the quarrel to get rid of Johanna so that she could wait out the Committee meeting alone, feeling that her usual bravado and cynicism were in danger of deserting her and not daring to allow the others to see her defenseless.

Trudy was scared. She knew this because all at once she found she could both read and concentrate. Both activities were impossible to her in her untroubled moments. She lay across her bed reading *The Catcher in the Rye* for the seventh time. It was far and away her favorite book, and she resorted to it at such moments in her life. The untrammelled dialogue soothed and sustained her; Holden Caulfield's restlessness and rebellion restored her faith in herself. . . . She too . . . then his hyperboles suddenly grew too outrageous, and she flung the paperback across the room where it landed on Johanna's bed, spewing pages as it travelled through the air. Now there was nothing to do but wait.

Trudy endured three minutes of silence and inactivity. Then she moved her hand slowly down her leg which was curled up before her and, after two trips of slow exploration she found the hard crust of an old scab. Carefully, with the precision born of years of careful practice, she began to remove it, slipping a fingernail under its edge, enjoying a flash of pain as she moved too close to the unhealed part. When the blood came she stopped temporarily, nursing the raw under-area, staunching the flow. The process absorbed her utterly. Each time she waited until the bleeding stopped and then, with the infinite skill of a great watchmaker, she returned to alter the tight arrangement of tissues above the old sore. As she worked at it the anticipated threats of the Disciplinary Committee faded, the neglect of Jamie Roebling for her, the heat in her room, dissolved. For that small space of time on the May Saturday afternoon Trudy Langer was happily at work at something which gave her moments of absolute pleasure.

Elizabeth Rankin's temper had not been improved by the trip up three steaming flights of stairs to Sophie's room. Puffing a little she knocked and then went quickly in before Sophie, stretched on her bed fully dressed and wrapped in her trench coat, had a chance to reply. The room was narrow and high, its peaked roof cut into an elevated triangle by a mahogany tie beam that reduced the little room to a normal rectangle.

"Are you ill?"

"No."

"Will you be free at four?"

"As free as I will be at any hour today. As free . . ." Sophie unconsciously countered Miss Rankin's hostility by rushing on, unleashing all the last days' accumulated bitterness, ". . . as I'll be this summer and next year from one end of it to the other. As free . . ."

"Good. Will you meet with the Disciplinary Committee in the Headmistress's Office at four?"

"Indeed I will. Delighted."

Miss Rankin turned to the door. She assumed the offhand air of a person who remembers at the last moment before departure that she has forgotten a most inconsequential matter and returns to mention it. "And, oh yes, one other thing, Miss Seward. Do you have Miss Acton's key to the stage?"

Sophie sprang up, dispersing by her precipitous action the calm, self-contained tone of satire she had managed to give her answers. Suddenly she was agitated by the clutter of her room and her utter inability to remember where she had left the key. The bureau . . . my sweater pocket . . . the zippered compartment of my purse . . .

Before Miss Rankin's fixed face, which seemed to be condemning all the procedures of her life in a single, blank, chicken-stare, Sophie rushed from one place to another, looking, turning over piles of clothes and paper, spilling, in her haste and because of the shaking in her hands, the contents of her purse onto the floor behind her bureau.

"I . . . can't seem to find it. I know it was here on the bureau last evening. . . . I saw it when I came in. Why? Does Ellen need it? For something right now?"

"No matter," said Miss Rankin, pleased with the outcome of her climb. Now it would be possible to put off the confrontation for a little time, to anticipate and plan the scene at four, without rushing into it thoughtlessly and thus wasting some of the force, the pleasure. "We'll meet at four?"

"Eight bells," said the captain's daughter, laughing foolishly with relief. Miss Rankin looked blankly at her for a moment, and left.

Lucy Moore felt the muscles in her back pulling, giving, relaxing and stretching again as her right arm swung in front of her, then violently behind, to return Robbie's balls. They'd been playing for a set and a half, Robbie enjoying the contest which she felt she had a good chance of winning, and Lucy relishing the simple delights of moving winter-bound muscles and tendons, the freedom a sleeveless shirt and shorts gave to a body that hated the confines of heavy, long, tight clothing.

A child of the sun since the age of four, Lucy found human complexities and mental miseries entirely incomprehensible. She was born in Gloucester where her parents had run a boat yard for twenty years before her birth. They were both simple, open, happy middle-aged people whose sole desire in life, an outdoor existence, had been completely satisfied by their occupation. From early April when, bundled in jackets, snow pants and scarves against the still-harsh ocean wind, they came out into the wan morning sun to begin cautiously uncovering parts of the boats in their care, to scrape and caulk and paint, until late in October when the last blocks were driven under grounded hulls and the final ropes and tarpaulins pulled taut and fastened, they never went indoors except to sleep and, when it rained, to eat, at a table pulled up close to the one large window in their sitting room so they could watch the sea as they ate charcoal-grilled, thick slabs of fish and drank their black coffee. They were quiet, even silent people whose lives were too full of small boats and the sea to leave any room for wider or, to them, lesser concerns. They were content to let Lucy run between the boats, chattering to the owners, intimate from the time she could walk, with men who loved the sea and approached it confidently, as a comrade, in their boats.

Lucy grew up to think of boats as part of their owners' families. She would say: "John Longely took *Sumter* and Jane and little Joe out for the day, about six this morning." This was in the years of her early teens when her parents left their house later in the morning—at eight—because Mrs. Moore had developed a touch of arthritis in her back. Her husband stayed behind in the weather-beaten shingled bungalow to help her out of bed.

For Lucy school was a dreaded interruption to the infinitely preferable world of sun-tanned people and sturdy boats, sea air and sun that the water front represented to her. Winter was death, spring the beginning of the real life, and summer its passionate height. But her quick mind learned what was expected of it, impatiently, so that it would be free to get back to the reality of the unlettered sea.

After her mother died (the little stitch in her back that had made getting up at six in the morning more and more difficult turned its malignant face after a few years of surreptitious, enervating activity and revealed itself as an incomprehensible cancer), Mike Moore and his daughter never achieved any understanding of how it could have happened. The family had always lived under the unstated dictum that a human being who pursued air and sun, lived close to sharp, cold, clear salt water, ate very little except the unadulterated, fresh products of the ocean and drank spring water, sometimes flavored with freshly ground coffee beans, must somehow be almost immortal. They were stunned by the blow to their deepest conviction that Mrs. Moore's death represented.

In her confusion Lucy reacted unexpectedly. She decided to leave Gloucester and go away to college. The school she chose specialized in training students to teach physical education. There, in her golden, scrubbed, bronzed and silent way, she was successful in the first, heavily academic year. But the temporary alliance with the things of the mind lasted only until halfway through her sophomore year. Little by little, during the hours of tennis and field hockey, basketball and lacrosse, she regained her old faith in the omnipotence of an easy, well-functioning body. When her father died in her senior year she was no longer vulnerable to the shock that she had felt at her mother's death, for now she had constructed a new equation of health with youth, and death, not with the sudden, vital failure of a system in full possession of its powers, but with old age. For as long as she lived Lucy Moore, who in July was to become the wife of a young athletic coach at Williams College, would never lose her distrust in the movements of a mind lodged in an inert or awkward or unaccomplished body. She was pledged irrevocably to a fraternity of the physical whose members flexed well-toned muscles for the pure joy of the act, sweated and strained in desperate games out of delight in them, and in anticipation of the added joy that came at the end with moments of absolute relaxation, took fantastic chances with wrists and biceps, clavicles and fibulae, nerve fibers and vertebrae.

At Miss Hands, her first school after practice teaching, Lucy was entirely happy. Miss Blount loved games too: the sight of her girls, their hair flying, their young voices raised to a desperate edge as they screamed instructions and demands at each other, their concentrating faces flushed and excited, gave her the comforting feeling that all was basically well with them. She cherished the belief that a hot, hard-fought game of hockey solved most intellectual conflicts for young persons and many psychical ones as well. The honors given at Miss Hands were mainly athletic awards—letters, numerals, cups, and publicly posted lists of varsity and junior varsity teams—and to all this emphasis upon the achievements of physical coordination Lucy gave pleased, silent assent. Unconsciously she shared Miss Blount's lifelong distrust of native intelligence and spectacular intellectual accomplishment, although she was ignorant of its origin in the Headmistress's personal history of determined struggle against the odds of a meager mental endowment and her years of supplementary training in progressive educational theories of the "well-rounded child." She was dimly aware that to the Headmistress athletics served as a gratifying and necessary source of recognition for the "non-academic" students whose "difficulties" with studies deserved to be ignored by a too-cerebral faculty while achievements on the ropes and rings—and in the big game against the Stratford Academy for Girls—merited high and vocal praise.

Lucy was grateful for the long afternoons at Miss Hands devoted to sports, for the beautiful fields that she kept filled with teams, practice sessions and competitive, intraschool games, for the boisterous support of the students who admired her ability to play everything with them. Her agility because she was "older" amazed them, and they never realized that she was, at most, four years their senior. The sun pouring, prematurely hot, down upon the tennis courts, the grass springing lush and green between white lines on the hockey field, John Fish of Williams waiting to dance with her week end after next in Springfield, a summer ahead of sand, sun and sailing out of Falmouth ("John and *Gadabout* and I") after their wedding, their life next year in a trailer (a clean, shining, slightly expanded symbol of the old locker room) while he finished his master's degree and they played tennis and golf in the afternoon, and bowled, and swam in the University pool in the evenings: at this moment in her life Lucy was completely happy and more fulfilled than she would ever be later when some of her dreams had had time to push themselves into reality. To her the oppressive gloom of this afternoon late in

May which so many of the weary faculty felt, the day laden with stringy tensions, end-of-year reports and Comments and tensely emotional students, was only theoretical, a figment of the faculty's collective, sedentary imagination. Serving her first ace in this set to Robbie, she shook her head ruefully, moved to the other court and carefully placed her left toe precisely at the service line. She lifted her left arm in a mighty arc and brought her racket down on the elevated ball. Smashing it into the court where Robbie stood waiting, with all the physical force of which she was capable, she felt a moment of intense, concentrated joy as the ball, perfectly placed, eluded Robbie's racket and bounced fair just inside the back line of the court.

"Thirty *love*," she called delightedly and raised her arm for the next serve.

On the drawing board, Mrs. Bache's sorrowful Jewish face, blocked in charcoal, looked heavy, almost doughy. This was not what Meg wanted at all. In disgust she scrubbed it out, scowled, squinted at her subject, and began again. Afraid to move, Mrs. Bache said out of tight lips: "How do you spell 'disturbing?' I or e?"

"I, I think. What is 'disturbing' or who?"

"In chemistry that dull senior Jenny Newmark. She is always a disturbing element. I don't understand why she is not dead."

"*Dead?*"

"She sucks at her thumb still, did you know?"

"I've noticed. But certainly *that* won't kill her."

"Yes. It does not matter what we are making, white phosphorus, copper sulphate hydrate, carbon disulphide. Right in the middle of the experiment she starts to suck at her thumb. I am relieved the labs are over. I thought I would be called to be the major witness at a state inquiry."

"Inquest," said Meg helpfully, squinting at the difficult line of Mrs. Bache's tired shoulders and slowly transferring what she found to the paper on the easel before her.

Meg had wanted to do a charcoal of Mrs. Bache's head all year. From across the room at endless faculty meetings, at the table in the Buttery, in the halls, she had watched her with interest, being not so much concerned with any verbal facts of autobiography as with the evident, infinite, age-old patience in her face; she itched to translate that weariness, the hint of some deep world-sickness in her eyes, to drawing paper and charcoal. She was not a head for pastels, Meg's favorite medium for Lucy Moore and students who, at seventeen were colored to fit the light, glowing boundaries of the crayons, but a natural charcoal, bleak, tired, giving way in her shoulders and arms, her neck and back of the head, to invisible and mortal pressures. Few persons on the faculty knew Mrs. Bache well. Her natural reticence, her often-expressed conviction that her personal confines in Faculty House were mysteriously intruded upon by others, and the squirrel-like frenzy with which she clasped her possessions to her, repulsed any faculty advances. Meg, by establishing a drawing-board bridge, was beginning at the very end of the year to know her a little.

Mrs. Bache wrote another Comment on the pad on her lap, trying not to move her head too much. For Gertrude Langer she wrote: "Could do better if she would place more emphasis on study. C—" Her cramped script took only a line in the large space provided and she felt worried about its inadequacy. She could think of nothing else to say.

"Emphasis or emphatic?" she asked.

"How is it used?"

" 'Emphasis on study.' "

"That's right. Who is this paragon?"

"No, no. Trudy Langer. She will not emphasis on study."

"Isn't that the truth. Did you also say she was a disturbing element? Or doesn't she suck her thumb?"

Mrs. Bache smiled wearily, and then quickly drew her mouth back into its posed set.

"I hardly know her. But from what Miss Blount tells me she is more disturbed than disturbing."

Meg thought of Ellen's overheard description of the new senior society of scurvy elephants and smiled at her model, both in recognition of the truth of her remark, and in silent thanks for her awareness of the responsibilities of posing. *How Trudy would hate that summary of herself, how gratified Miss Blount would be by its clear compassion, how little we all really know of each other. I'm lucky to be able to fall back on the pictorial aspects of the human soul for my creative satisfactions. Now and then I catch a fleeting glimpse of it, without having to explore it with lethal words or transfer it to a murderous clef staff. I am translating a five-dimensional thing to a one-dimensional scale and I'm lucky it's a relatively simple procedure, like removing a wart in comparison to an open-heart operation. Anything more complex than the wart I would be frightened of.*

"That was miserable last night in the sitting room, wasn't it?" asked Meg, more to relax Mrs. Bache's slowly tensing back muscles into their customary droop than to make small talk.

"I don't know. I went early to bed." Then, feeling that her constant weariness needed further explication, she said, "It was hard. The last day and the girls breaking everything they touched. All that cleaning up of the lab afterwards. What happened?"

"The play—did you see it?"

"No. My English is not advanced enough for Shakespeare."

"It was a fiasco, in any language. They gave Sophie a rough time."

Even to Mrs. Bache's elementary command of the language the referent of the pronoun was entirely clear. "They are hard on failure here. I've felt it myself many times," she said.

"They are harder on success, I think. I remember a history teacher some years back whose classroom during her free periods was always crowded with students talking to her, asking her questions, debating, laughing. Her name was mentioned in a number of letters from parents commending the school for their daughter's fine backgrounds and preparation in history once they got to college. She was replaced, as soon as Miss Blount could find an alumna of Miss Hands just graduated from Bryn Mawr with, I believe, a major in philosophy. But the new lady *had* taken a course there once in medieval history."

"Is that so?"

"It is." Meg squinted again, standing away from the portrait, trying to ascertain the exact slant of Mrs. Bache's jaw line which she had made too taut, too brisk.

"Miss Seward will never suffer for that trouble. She is not coming back, is she?"

"I don't think so, no."

Still writing Comments in her crabbed German script, Mrs. Bache felt a pang of pleasure in her own unaccustomed security, and then repressed it as ignoble, unworthy. She had signed her contract for next year on the day it was offered to her. The perpetual quarry must always feel this a little, being just for the moment safe, holed up, aware of the hunt going by hot in pursuit of another prey. . . .

"What will she do?"

"I have no idea." Now the line of the jaw was down, satisfactory, a *ding an sich*, pure and beautiful, suggesting much more than it was, a lifetime witness to horrors, the prey escaped into late evening protection of the forest, and yet with all its connotations a fine, exact, fitting thing in itself. *I must do Sophie*, she thought. *Another victim but that one Elizabethan, suffering from the inside out, inviting catastrophe and attack after the inner softening up. Can I get a line for that palsy in her hands, and another, different kind for the instability of her head? Oils might do it.* . . .

Mrs. Bache broke in upon her planning. "She's had a long history of teaching, hasn't she?"

"Long and varied."

"And now another move?"

"So it seems. Not that I think it will solve her problems.

I don't quite see her as a teacher somehow. She's too sensitive, too . . . too lacking in stamina. Not made for the slings and arrows of teaching."

"No, but then I do not think many of us are, do you?"

Meg laughed softly. "You're right. But with Sophie it's more complex. She is always sure that in the next place it will be different, she will be different, she will find her profession and be comfortable."

"I think she will not, ever."

"No. You can run, as someone said about this architectural abomination we're in, but you can't hide."

A rap, repeated, brought Trudy abruptly to her feet. Miss Rankin stood at her door.

"We'd like to see you in Miss Blount's office in about ten minutes, Miss Langer."

"All right, Miss Rankin."

After Miss Rankin closed the door behind her, Trudy stood, still staring at it, and then mumbled viciously: "I come, Graymalkin." And Miss Rankin, walking briskly down the corridor of Elias Cook Hall, suddenly recalled the thin stream of blood running down Trudy's leg and wondered what she had done to it.

Jo Long waved to Robbie Parks on the tennis court, turned into the sidewalk leading to Faculty House—Ellen seemed to be asleep under Eighty-Eight so she did not disturb her—and went up to her room, despite the heat taking two steps at a time. She stood looking at her face in her mirror: *the boredom of another session of that damnable committee.* The heat in her room was intolerable; she had forgotten to lower the shade when she left in the morning and the sun had touched and heated, almost inflamed, every object in the room. Sighing at her defenselessness against it, she stripped, put on a white terrycloth robe and went down the hall to the bathroom. Standing under the cold shower which streamed down over her head she shook her saturated hair, scrubbed her wet scalp hard with her fingernails and felt, for the first time today, totally at peace with herself.

At her desk, Miss Blount read her mail. It was always sparse on Saturday. No secretaries worked on the week ends so she had the rare enjoyment of opening the envelopes herself. Never would she have asked a secretary to leave her first-class mail unopened, for she was not consciously aware of this childish pleasure of hers in slipping the knife into the envelope, slitting it neatly, slipping the always-promising enclosure out, but it was true: being Headmistress and having a secretary cut her off from a delight she had always felt as a girl at school receiving few letters . . . the moment of suspense . . . *it might be anything.* Deftly she opened the first letter. A late acceptance, at long last, for Trudy Langer from Mitford College, where she'd been on the waiting list. *Good. That will be a help with her father when he arrives for Commencement. I must tell her at once.*

The next letter contained a second envelope enclosed within it. *A wedding. Oh nice.* She slipped the engraved letter out of its blank envelope, the tissue protecting the expensive-looking print floating to the floor. *Eleanor Ames, in Bridgeport, July 28th. Perhaps if someone else from Boston is going and I can get a ride down . . .* The Headmistress wrote the date and the event on her THINGS TO DO pad and picked up the next letter: "Dear Miss Blount: I am writing to inquire about the possibility of entering my daughter Felice . . ."

Slowly the Disciplinary Committee reassembled. Ellen stood in the entryway to Arts Hall watching students stream out of

Elias Cook. Dressed for town, half of them wore straight, tight khaki skirts and dark paisley shirts, the collars buttoned down, the sleeves rolled in two-inch cuffs from the elbow. Their legs were bare and to a girl they wore flat, black, soft shoes. The other half, Ellen decided, were walking to a soda shop not far from the school's gates: khaki bermuda shorts, colored shirts whose collars flapped over the tops of sweatshirts (*in this weather!*), on which MISS HANDS SCHOOL FOR GIRLS was printed in bold block letters.

Ellen walked back into the office and sat down in her old place at the coffee table. Miss Blount was still at her desk reading her mail. Jo arrived, shedding water from her wet curls at each step. Sitting down she immediately picked up a pencil as if to indicate to the others that she was not only ready to begin but was in fact almost finished with her end of the business and ready to be excused. Miss Blount opened the last letter neatly ("Dear Principal: There is no doubt that our great new series of Video-Audio tapes has been greeted with enthusiasm by educators everywhere . . ."), dropped it into her wastebasket and joined the teachers at the tables.

"It is just four," she said.

"Where's Miss Rankin?" asked Jo, not without some pleasure at this rare opportunity to note a defect in the assistant's ordinarily impeccable personal scheduling.

"Shall we start without her? She'll be along any moment," said Ellen.

"No. We'll wait," said Miss Blount. She frowned at Jo's impatience. It was not that she wished to prolong the whole distasteful business, but rather that she feared to take any steps which the assistant, with her stronger logic, would later, and publicly, find it necessary to countermand.

Trudy Langer, coughing lightly to introduce her presence, stood in the doorway to the Office: "Miss Rankin said you wanted to see me."

"She *did?*" said Ellen in an astonished tone, before she

realized how decisive her question must have sounded to Trudy.

"Just wait outside for a moment, Trudy. We'll be with you in a moment," said the Headmistress.

"Are we all here now?" Miss Blount shut the door.

"We are," said Miss Rankin. "And I've asked Miss Seward to come in for a few moments. She ought to be here by now."

"Why?" asked Ellen, "and why Trudy Langer?"

"Miss Acton," Elizabeth Rankin turned to her, "you seem, as usual, to be in favor of doing nothing, about anything. I asked Miss Langer so we could find out how she came to have a key to the stage door. I asked Miss Seward so we could discover just when she came into possession of Trudy's paper. Are you in favor of dropping both these matters now? Before you thought Trudy ought to be guillotined at the very least."

Ellen's temper gave way at once. "I thought that if it were proven she cheated she ought to be punished, not guillotined as it pleases you to suggest. But I am willing to accept Miss Seward's testimony as it stands. I do not think we should challenge her in this committee."

"Why not, pray?"

"Because . . . because she's upset and . . . for any of us to show further distrust of her would upset her further."

"But you are willing to upset Trudy Langer," interposed Miss Blount, "by questioning her?"

"Yes, if necessary, although I doubt if we'd upset her very much. But there seems to be no point to that. Trudy's convenient little explanation is probably solidified by now so that we won't get the truth from her. As they say in the movies, she's had time to prepare her defense."

"Shall we call her in?" asked Miss Rankin, ignoring Ellen pointedly and looking at the Headmistress.

Miss Blount opened the door. "Come in, Trudy." Her voice was reassuring, gentle.

It was not at Miss Blount that Trudy looked as she sat

down at the coffee table but at Miss Rankin. She seemed unwilling to take her eyes from her, as if she feared that losing sight of her would be dangerous and place her at a distinct disadvantage.

"Trudy," said the Headmistress, cushioning the proceedings with compassionate sounds before Miss Rankin could retrieve her command. "You remembered that incident with Miss Seward about—the quiz?"

O holy Saint Gregory, thought Ellen. *The incident.*

"Yes, Miss Blount."

"This committee has a further question about it."

"Yes."

"Miss Langer," Miss Rankin's sharp voice broke in upon the air of amiability that the Headmistress's soft questions and Trudy Langer's agreeable answers had created. "How soon after that English quiz began did Miss Seward discover your paper?"

"I can't possibly remember that, Miss Rankin."

"Why not?"

"Well, it was a pretty short quiz, you know, and we were all sort of thrown off when we discovered that Miss Seward was proctoring it in Miss Acton's place. . . ."

"Why would that throw you all off, Trudy?" asked Ellen.

"Well, Miss Acton, you know how queer she is, always dropping things and dashing across the room with those jerky movements when you least expect her. She makes us nervous . . .

And that to move is not always to be alive, thought Ellen.

"So I guess we fooled around a bit when she was giving the papers out and she counted them off wrong so that Livvy Evans didn't get a paper and raised her hand. And then Miss Seward got red and shaky and couldn't find the test papers, oh, you know how she is, Miss Acton."

"But Miss Langer, notwithstanding Miss Seward's personal idiosyncracies, you *did* bring a written copy of the Hamlet soliloquy that I asked you to memorize to class with you, did you not?"

"No, I did not. That copy I wrote out in class and then copied."

"I've taught you English for two years, Trudy. I've never known you to be that careful about what you handed in before."

Trudy's nose burned red, and her long braid of yellow hair seemed suddenly too wet and too heavy for her head. Slow blotches of fiery color made their way up her neck. She looked as if she were in acute physical distress, as if her body was visibly displaying what inwardly she was feeling in order to invoke some measure of sympathy for her inner state. "This time," she said with harsh insistence, "I was."

There was a knock on the door. Miss Blount pulled her desk chair over to the table, and gestured to Miss Seward to be seated.

"Come to the circle," murmured Ellen, smiling at Sophie.

"What was that?" asked Miss Rankin, her suspicions always aroused by curious allusions.

"Nothing," replied Ellen, "Just something they used to say to us in kindergarten."

"Miss Seward," began Miss Rankin who wanted to eliminate all the slackness that had now developed in the lines of the meeting. "At what point during the quiz you were administering to the seniors a few weeks ago did you find the paper of Miss Langer's you claim was a crib-sheet?"

"At what point? What do you mean?"

"I mean, when?"

"Soon after we'd started, do you mean that?"

"Well yes, but how soon? Immediately?"

As Sophie sought desperately among these choices for some memory of what, in her mind, had become a confused morass, her hands began their jerky little dance, as if they were puppets separate from her wrists and capable of a life of their own. She said: "She had it all the while . . . I'm certain of that—just look at the careful, cramped handwriting, in order to get the whole thing on a very small, inconspicuous piece of paper . . . but there was some confusion in the room, about one student who didn't have a question paper, so by the time she got it and I got back to the desk and saw Trudy, it was . . . some time . . . after the start of the quiz." Sophie's voice trailed off until the last words died, as if they accompanied her realization that her accusation had just now been dealt a lethal blow.

The committee members gazed at Trudy. She was looking at Miss Rankin and smiling a crooked little smile which seemed to be lit strangely from each side by her blotched skin. She uttered a final sentence with the air of a fencer delivering a *coup de grâce:* "I wrote on that tiny piece of paper, Miss Rankin, because that was all the scratch paper I had with me at the time."

"I see," said Miss Rankin.

Trudy turned to Miss Seward and smiled triumphantly. Ellen could not bear the tableau any longer. "I think Miss Langer may be excused now, don't you, Miss Rankin, while we discuss the matter further," she said.

As Trudy opened the door, the Headmistress called: "Oh Trudy, I forgot. I've some good news for you. Your acceptance from Mitford came through this morning. You'll have a letter in your box Monday, if it's not already there. We are all so pleased for you. And, Trudy, put something on that leg."

The case rests, thought Ellen. Trudy looked relieved and thanked the Headmistress. She said she would.

"Will you wait outside for a few moments, Trudy," said Miss Rankin.

"I see no point in pursuing this," said Miss Rankin. "It seems clear that there is no evidence one way or another. Miss Seward is not certain of the time and Trudy unfortunately is. But the question of the key remains. Have you found yours, Miss Seward?"

"No . . . no. I've looked everywhere. It was on the bureau after the play, I know, but . . . I seem . . . to have mislaid it now."

"Not mislaid it. Trudy Langer and her cohorts used it this morning to smoke backstage."

"Oh *no.* How did she get my key?"

"We'll ask her."

Called back so quickly, before she had time to relish her first clear victory, Trudy was clearly unprepared for the question Miss Rankin shot at her. But success had sharpened her reflexes and even more, her ability to feel the direction the wind was blowing and to gauge its precise velocity. Instinctively she knew that having established her lie as truth she was now in a strong position to add anything she wished to it without danger of detection. So keenly were her senses attuned to the atmosphere in the room that she felt safe in attacking, like a barnyard fowl joining her mates to set upon a sick chicken. The telltale flush dying away along her cheek bones, a thin stream of blood running down the side of her leg from the sore she had just reopened, she told the committee that Miss Seward had given her the key.

"I don't believe that," said Ellen at once.

"You . . . you terrible, terrible girl. You lie—and lie. You . . ." Sophie was incoherent in her fury, tears in her eyes, her head shaking so that her hair sprang onto her cheeks. She would have gone on but Miss Blount saw the danger of this display, and told Trudy to leave. Ellen went out with her, but she felt unable to trust herself to speak to her. She brought back a paper cup full of water for Sophie who was now shaking uncontrollably. Her voice had deserted her, and she was speaking in a coarse whisper, saying over and over: "No. No. No. No. No."

"Miss Acton, will you take Miss Seward to her room?" said Miss Rankin. Her pleasure at the end to which this meeting had come showed clearly through her words of concern for the teacher.

Sophie whispered: "Miss Blount, you can't believe that . . ."

"What I believe matters not at all at this point," replied the Headmistress grandly, now in full control. "I think perhaps we could forestall all this unpleasantness in the future by having only one key to the doors in this Hall, kept in the Guidance Office and under Miss Rankin's responsibility. In that way the fire hazard ought to be considerably diminished," she finished what she considered a little joke, to lighten the atmosphere.

Ellen left with Sophie. Jo, who had sat through the whole meeting staring at the coffee table in a state of acute embarrassment at the displays of emotion, said, in order to have something to say: "What was that all about?"

"I'll tell you," said Miss Rankin. She sounded exultant, and she was. Through the haze that the spilled emotion left in the room she had sensed a solution, one that fitted her way of thinking perfectly and was, she felt sure, an explanation for the whole murky situation.

Ellen came back into the room, shaken. "She wanted to go alone," she said to no one at all, and sat down again.

"Trudy Langer could never have stolen that key, or anyone else for that matter. I was in that room today, and it is so totally disorganized and upset that no one could find anything there let alone a student who didn't know her way around it or where anything might be kept."

"How did she get it then?" asked Jo, audibly tired of the whole affair.

"Sophie Seward *did* give it to her," replied Elizabeth Rankin with the air of a herald announcing an unexpected victory to the troops.

Everyone looked at her.

"Yes. Gave it to her. Gave it to her in order to incriminate her. She knew those girls smoked back there, she knew Trudy would use the key and be caught, and that when the matter of the quiz came up here Trudy would be further discredited by the discovery that she and the others had broken the smoking rule. Trudy was telling the truth. She's told the truth all along. Miss Seward is the sort of person who must feel she is being persecuted. She's felt that all along about the students, and this latest maneuver is in line with everything else."

She's certain, thought Ellen: *it's exactly what she would have done. So she's absolutely certain.*

"I cannot help but agree with you," murmured the Headmistress.

There was silence, as if the others were weighing the new-found unity between the Headmistress and her assistant. Ellen said then: "Miss Blount, would I be right in assuming that even if we had found that Trudy had done what she was accused of there would have been a good many good reasons for our doing nothing about it?"

"Reasons?"

"Reasons, Miss Blount, that always seem to weigh heavily here when a student's word is judged against a teacher's. Financial reasons, to which I am not entirely insensitive, liking to be paid, but which nevertheless influence many decisions; psychological reasons—it's so much easier and pleasanter to defend the student and avoid trouble with her parents than to defend the teacher who is, after all, an easily expendable thing. Moral reasons even—"

"Miss Acton," said Miss Rankin.

"Miss Acton," said the Headmistress at the same time, ominously. "Are you saying that I have acted immorally in this affair?"

Like a saboteur who rests on a hilltop for a moment to survey the damage he has just left behind him, Ellen took stock. And she found that, like Macbeth, in whose bloody wake she had just finished dragging twenty-three reluctant juniors, she had gone so far now "that, should I wade no more Returning were as tedious as go o'er." *I have come to the circle for the first time in my adult life and I shall say my piece, although it may cost me a good deal.*

"I am saying"—Ellen stood up as if distance from the little group around the coffee table would provide force for her words. She leaned back against Miss Blount's bookcase and folded her arms—"that we do these girls a great injustice when we allow them to think that there are degrees of honesty. We do them a grave wrong when we hesitate to be hard when they err slightly, when we say 'they are young, and we cannot stigmatize them.' Or when we say the even more terrible thing, 'everyone lies or cheats or steals sometime and we cannot single out just one offender.' If everyone cheats and lies then the best thing we can do for them here, far better than teaching them Advanced Algebra or the History of Science, is to set every one who does these things straight, here, now, before the costly lessons of the adult world are learned at far greater mental anguish than the small school world affords. If we make them suffer here that is too bad, but we have inoculated them against the next exposure, and that is part of our job as teachers . . ."

Now everyone was standing, except Jo. The Headmistress and her assistant both looked distracted, almost dazed, as if they were no longer listening to Ellen and were reviewing in their minds what it was they each wished to say when she finished.

" . . . and one last thing. We who teach in small private schools with little or no endowments, or you who administer them, are truly hirelings. We are in the awful position of having to placate and please and satisfy the customer and his agents. But in this matter of training the human mind and molding the human spirit we cannot allow ourselves to be comfortable in the posture of hirelings. There is only one right, not the right for the rich and another for the not-so-rich, one easy right for the young and another harsher one for the mature, one half-right that works for quizzes and little tests, and a nice rounded whole one that serves for a unit test. . . ."

The Headmistress turned white. Her fury was so great that she could not speak.

"That's enough. We don't have to listen to this sort of insult. Miss Blount . . ." said Miss Rankin, echoing what clearly was in the Headmistress's inarticulate mouth to say.

". . . and it's up to us to make certain they understand *there is no distinction,*" finished Ellen, knowing her time had run out and that her audience could no longer be held quiet.

Now Miss Rankin had found the proper words: "Miss Acton, you are out of order!"

Ellen smiled. "Miss Rankin, no one could be more aware of that, at this moment, than I."

"It must be almost dinner time," said Jo. Now she felt she hated Ellen for calling out her allegiance which she disliked enlisting in this manner, and she hated the others for allowing Ellen to go so far that they were all now caught in a tangle of words from which they might never free themselves.

"It is. If there is no further business . . ." said Miss Rankin, her voice too high for comfort.

"No further business that *I* know of," said the Headmistress. She sounded weak and tired.

The closeted session had exhausted even her endless vitality. She opened her door and breathed deeply of the hall air uncontaminated by the disturbing talk that had raged in her office. She nodded coldly as Ellen passed in front of her, and then again abruptly, to Jo. Miss Rankin stayed behind to work on Monday's schedule with the Headmistress. Ellen and Jo left the building together.

"Interesting meeting, wasn't it?" asked Jo, and grinned at Ellen.

"Edifying," replied Ellen, and felt a twinge of distant, reverberant memory.

From Ellen's notebook for May— 196—:

Found written in a returned copy of *Macbeth* yesterday: "New slogan to replace *Quand Même* on shields, walls, letterheads and blazers of Miss Hands School for Girls: 'EVERYTHING NOT FORBIDDEN IS COMPULSORY.'" Taken from T. E. White, I think: *The Once and Future King*. I wonder if Liz Rankin would approve such a change.

You never dry the inside of beer glasses, Jo informed me as we had our usual Sunday evening six-pack in Robbie's room. I found this mysterious and questioned her, and she confessed that the reason escaped her, but if you *do* dry them, she claims, the beer poured into them is immediately flattened. I suspect this is folklore but Jo is devoted to its truth.

Flaubert: "Speech is a rolling machine that always stretches the feelings it expresses."

The itch for books to read is, to the lonely literate, like drugs or drink or to some few, sex. I have noticed that as I approach the final pages of one book I begin to look around desperately for the next. I can never go away for a day without taking a book with me to finish and another, in reserve, to begin, in case I should not be home in time. And the gap without one is unthinkable.

What is this strange panic at the thought of being left with nothing to read? The fear of the intellectual addict to be thrown back upon himself, his own words or in my case perhaps, on the book I have always thought I would write. Other people's books in an unending stream are a good substitute for one of one's own that was never written.

"No bomb that ever burst/Shatters the crystal spirit." "Poem on an Italian Soldier."

Today I came upon a description of an aboriginal tribe in the bush country in Australia who are capable of self-euthanasia. When a tribe member becomes convinced that he is dying, or for some reason wishes to die, he lies down and by some mysterious, potent lessening of vitality so formidable that the blood slowly ceases, the heart beat fibrillates, the eyes close, the whole tone of muscle becomes weak, and he dies, slowly, surely, he dies. We too do this, I suppose, in a less dramatic way in civilized countries: old men and women die soon after retirement, some psychotics a week after incarceration, unhappy young children institutionalized for too long. . . .

Coming back from Mass the other day at eight. The Headmistress going to breakfast. Pleasant, full of vague smiles. She greeted me and then asked me where I'd been so early on a

Sunday morning. A walk? she asked. "To Mass." "Oh," she said in her surprised, amiable way, "Do you still keep that up?"

The Twins in the Buttery today after lunch. Like a married couple after long association they begin to look and act alike. Standing together at the ice-cream cooler, both digging in to their elbows. I watched as they came up at the same moment each with a candy bar in her right hand, wrapped in purple paper, called *Sidewalk Malteds*. One of them might have emerged with a *Creamside*, but no. . . . They stood eating the bars at the window of the Buttery. Each with her left hand on her hip. Their eyes engaged absolutely with each other . . . *qui fata trahunt retrahuntque sequamur*: whither the fates in their ebb and flow, draw us, let us follow. Vergil, *Aeneid* V, 709. Robbie pointed this out to me in her textbook during Chapel this morning.

I would have become a writer instead of eternally planning to be one or expecting that someday I would turn to it, except for one great fault: all of my life I have noticed very little of what went on around me. Now at forty, when it is almost too late, I find I can watch five pigeons on a roof's edge, all facing their foolish heads and triangular bodies in the same direction (like spectators at a tennis match) although there is nothing visible to me for them to be focusing on so intently. Or Millicent waiting for her bus in the evening as I take my pre-prandial walk *away* from Arts and Faculty and Elias Cook and all else. She talks to herself—I think she must be arguing with the cook with whom she is dumb when she is in her presence—and then she performs a delicate little arabesque around the telephone pole. After a little she rests against it, addressing it coyly, then dances back the other way, as if unwinding. What is she telling it? Whom does she see it as? I find I am pushing myself into her, trying to peer out of her mad, deluded eyes. Another pigeon joins the five, alighting from the originality of its flight and settling into the same conformist stance as the others. Now I notice everything, too late.

CHAPTER V

Faculty House

AND can I face it out once more? Revealed to the universal eye as a coward and a weakling, thought to be mad vicious incompetent, can I rally again, put on my uniform from which this time the buttons and badges and other signs of rank have been removed, take up my sightless rifle and go back again? Where in all this continuous round of classrooms offices faculty bathrooms smoking rooms butteries dining rooms cafeterias little bedrooms (cells?) hot plates gymnasiums sour locker rooms whispering libraries steel files halls blackboards did I misplace Miss Sophie Seward Mrs. Louis Larkin who thought once she could somewhere somehow make a peace treaty with a way of life and coexist with it without breaking out in an acne of despair an orgy of shaking without crying and running away without mistaking intentions misunderstanding laughter without seeing faces that mocked beneath a layer of skin, backs that curved in disgust shoulders that raised and lowered with indifference.

Is it I alone? Am I running, a courier from a defeated front, against a world of people in a comfortable snug current that finds its bed and cuts deep and settles in, everyone but me. The school is a world like any other: the world of the ship my father knew and loved and strode through with such belligerent ease and the world men make together in foxholes or jails which for a time seem more real than home, preferable to, safer than any other place on earth. And monasteries, convents: these are single worlds in which one sex exists under some kind of communal peace treaty with itself and within it one human being no matter how poorly equipped for living can seemingly survive. Colette wrote of a world like this that she knew of in her youth, the world backstage at music halls at the beginning of the century. . . . Where did I put that collection? Oh here. "This crowd of women reacted like a barometer to any vagary of the weather . . . it was only latent hysteria; a kind of school-girl neurosis which afflicts women who are arbitrarily and point-lessly segregated from the other sex." Like me she sees the current overflow run muddy meander away from its rut and founder alone on dry ground.

I live an existence bordered by *if it had only been different and if that had only not happened.* Always only. Is this true of other people? Is there any way of finding out, contacting them for information, learning if their surfaces are, like quicksand, deceptive, their quiet desperation lurking always just under the smiling face and the humorous, offhand wave of the hand. Would marriage have helped me? Not the fact, but the emotional confines that living in such an arrangement must set up for someone like me whose nervous system seems to have been applied afterwards, just too late, to the physical components. Might it have ordered the jangling controlled the palsy systematized and subdued the discordant and chaotic plasm that boils up and over in me whenever the word is sharp or the look too long or the laughter edged with . . . with something. My nerves are so honest, so extroverted, they refuse to disguise themselves with the calm of the surface. They take over the shell and reduce it to bits of matter perpetually in motion and so even the appearance of fitting in of agreement of moving contentedly in the current (Ellen has this appearance, I think) is denied to me.

And my defeats have been so petty . . . by a girl in a moth-eaten purple tunic and badly-run tights who mouths great sentences with the air of a clown and pretends that the whole play is nothing but a long sneer aimed and carried down through the centuries against me alone . . . by a University fop who demanded of me what I could not give and what I learned too late he could not in any case have received . . . by an old lady who readily accepted symbols for blood and bone . . . by a hollow man who loved braid and water . . . by a hollow young boy, whose nerves and heart were all condensed on his leprous skin . . . by a dead marine who didn't cry out as he sank . . . by a loudmouthed senior in a Barn . . . by a woman with a voice of tin and great clusters of purple beads at her ears . . . a wooden leg in a golden body . . . a woman who loves another too much to persist in kindness . . . a bleeding scab. Mice crammed in my mouth I run the obstacle course always backwards, upstairs and downstairs my son John. . . .

My son John my single act of creation and even that a gross misshapen failure a defeat in the womb a departure from human form into grotesquerie a crossing of species for his benefit and mine alone so that a little human hopefully called John is born like a tadpole or a merman a fantastic imaginary unbelievable creature coming only to me whose nerves curled and strained and involuted to create a monster a throwback to prehistory when we were painfully rising from the sea before the psalmist looked over the green world and sang of his pristine delight "Oh Lord I love the beauty of your house, the dwelling place of your glory." There is no room in the inn for the monstrous John, and I, the monstrous bearer, have had some trouble signing the register.

Ellen has a faith—where does one find such a thing? Shall I search, or like the rat in the drawer will it suddenly horrifyingly appear to me at night in the dark with little scratching sounds and will I stand pat and be grateful or run as I've always run before or as they've run from me down the labyrinthine ways, joy of man's desiring, in terror at its approach? If I could believe I might be less vulnerable better protected less the victim and just for once in my piety and holy practices and prayers the victimizer or at the very least the neutral bystander. Does faith give believers an edge? Am I the object of every cruel humor because I am like some microbiological organism without a confining wall leaking out and running off in all directions? Can I be brought back and reunited on some principle, reassembled like the Christmas toys of children, reassigned like a soldier to some higher purpose that will permit me to ignore the mice the laughter the pointed vicious attack and the secret silent creeping one to become one with myself? Somehow I doubt it.

I watch people with faith in God and saints and spirits that descend. The very few that I know. Faith turns their sympathies in upon themselves and away from you and curbs and limits them to other members of the fold the lodge-members and pewholders and to all the supernatural coterie. I remember a woman who knelt for hours before the statue of a chromatic saint perpetualized in stone put flowers at its feet and paid for monster candles to put at its pedestal who walked away fast and back into her house and shut the door when a neighbor child was sick in her driveway. I am that sick child retching at my disgust vomiting along the restricted paths of the quadrangle while they the U's the belongers the joined the emotional haves warm and together and safe apply and test their Christianity only on themselves.

Has God, if He is, deserted me? Have I deserted Him if He is? Why have I in my greatest need always felt farthest from Him as if He would not permit my fright if He was? Is. Why do I feel cut away from any vital spring from the open heart like a tail severed from the body of a reptile which still moves and jerks? I am Mann's life's delicate child no home not even a lean-to or a cave or a hole. Are there true shelters on earth, any truer than the astronaut's capsule or the chamber of the nautilus or is everyone like me exposed to the mortal blasts of human irritation and impatience, the flaying by temper and scorn, the assault by narrowed eye lids and furiously set jaw the siege of the clenched fist? How does the human like the arthropod acquire a shell to keep it safe from fright and hurt? This too I need to know as well as the approaches to God although they may well be the same answer not for saints but for ordinary Christians endowed with a stronghold of pride and self-concern.

I am frightened by everything by what I cannot see but can only sense by oddity by perversion by the lump the sharp pain the spot of blood. Imperfect and malfunctioning as it is I rely too heavily upon the integrity of my body, having nothing else. I am panicked when it gives the least sign of possible failure. I have lain awake long nights extending the little leg pain the chest ache the stiffened neck the curious itch in the face into the fatal blood clot the nubbin of abnormal cells which even as I lay sleepless and throbbing terrified, expands into a cancer an ulcer a mortal growing horror that will crawl and spread to all the organs until my body is a great painful mass of diffused multiplied pain. The clutch at the heart the stitch in the side or the left arm which in the deep night becomes to my sleepless lidless mind the coronary the first anginous attack the hemorrhage which will attack in a moment while I lie alone and defenseless beneath sheets. Every ache is for me the beginning of total disorder and the stroke of disease. I catch fear of everything within my body from old wives' tales from hospital narratives brought back by friends who visit the sick with this in mind, from letters from novels and plays and newspapers. I hug them to my breast secretly in order to be prepared to anticipate to feel the very first moment of onslaught in the night the beginning of the end. . . .

I am the Lottery ticket marked with the black dot that signifies the beginning of the stoning by the villagers. Have this faculty and these students gathered their stones and piled them up ready for the throw? Am I Joseph K caught in a frozen sea around me the dangling man the Outsider the Lonely Hunter the beast of prey? Will I choose outrageous fortune, the door to the Tiger burning bright in the forests of the night? Can I ever play the main part the star the leading lady of even the smallest skit or is my impoverished ego so named by Sigmund

Freud doomed to stand-in understudy substitute breathing whimpers not bangs the eternal havenot underprivileged minority the babe in the wood the exposed on the hillside the emotional paraplegic the nothing nowhere behind the irrevocable rent in the black curtain the unrecognizable body recovered from the rubble on the vestibule to the shelter

"Where are you going now? I'm starved, aren't you?" Jo mopped her forehead, pushing away the damp hair.

"I ought to go up to see Sophie. She's probably still upset."

"Yes, I suppose." But neither of them made a move toward Faculty House. Jo wanted to find Robbie, and to eat. And Ellen, ever since they'd left the Headmistress's office, had been fighting her fear. In a spasm of remembering, stimulated by the unexpected word that had leaped unsummoned to her tongue, she was reliving her objections, her antagonism that her mother, waiting in her endless patience, had always aroused in her, and the fear. . . . Suddenly it was Mrs. Acton who needed her reassurance, on the third floor of Faculty House, and suddenly it was impossible for her to go home even once more.

"Let's clean up at the Buttery and wait for the others," said Jo.

Ellen said: "Let us go you and I when the evening is spread out against the sky like a patient etherized upon a table. . . ."

"What patient?" asked Jo.

"Thomas Stearns Eliot, you university illiterate," said Ellen affectionately. Together, held together by a new bond born of mutual retreat from unpleasantness, they started for the Buttery.

And so it happened that Meg Miers, coming upstairs just before the dinner carillon sounded, to ask Sophie where she'd put the small flats she'd used for *The Merchant* last night (Miss Blount wanted them repainted with summer flowers for the side of the stage at Commencement and she had bloody little time to paint summer flowers) found her hanging, dead, from the mahogany rafter in her room, her trench-coat belt knotted around her black throat. Meg in a shocked frenzy stumbled across the room, almost falling over the chair lying on its side and the huge Bible collapsed on the floor. She hardly knew she was climbing onto the bed and with a fierce jerk opening the belt. She had no strength left to catch the falling Sophie. Like a grotesque and oversized marionette, her face covered with a bloody acne of suffocation, an image of pure horror by Dürer (Doré? Daumier? Blake? no) she fell into a stiff heap, one foot resting, distorted, on the open Bible. Meg picked her up and laid her on the bed. Her trench coat had been tightly buttoned up to her neck as if she had been eager to emphasize the definitive closure of belt and coat beneath her chin. Mechanically Meg opened it: *how foolish, what good will it do?* The coat made her look shrunken, like a small, thin child in borrowed clothes. Her shoes had fallen off as she had kicked away the chair and the Bible which she must have added to reach the elevated rafters. Meg picked up the shoes (*loafers, they're called—how terrible!*) and slipped them easily onto the already withered and bloodless dead feet. From her smock pocket she took a scissors and cut the belt away from the black throat, gashing her palm as she did so. For one agonizing moment Meg stared at the blackened, swollen face, the eyes forced almost out of their sockets, the nose bulbous and blue with blood, the lips outraged, having split their bounds and formed a black oval at the bottom of the face, and the cheeks and chin violated tragically by the tongue like a bloated, burned sausage. Then, feeling sick, even as she cold-bloodedly, mechanically, professionally recorded what she had seen, Meg pulled the spread over the ghastly face. And before she went to the doorway, finally to give way to her horror, to scream for the others to come, she had time to memorize the rude final posture of the tongue and cheeks, as if, she thought, Sophie had in her last consciousness made this defiant black mouth as a final bloody gesture against them all.

CHAPTER VI

Emergency Meeting: Faculty House

THE heat had risen, leaving the campus heavy and sodden with fog. At nine in the evening little pockets of heat still lingered in the corners of rooms and at the edge of buildings. Millicent in a coat with a large fox collar which she wore summer and winter because her pride in the possession of the fur would not allow her to put it away when it grew warm, walked out through the gate, inserting into her stride an occasional little skip. She nodded goodnight to Mister Sam, the groundskeeper. He put up the chain behind her and said goodnight glumly. In a moment she had disappeared into the fog, on her way to the corner to wait for her bus.

Mister Sam continued his rounds. He walked close to the wall and every two or three feet flashed his light into the fog. He felt oddly uncertain tonight, disconcerted by the events of the past hour, the unannounced, sudden arrival of the coroner's car from Newton. Hard upon that, the town ambulance howling through the fog had almost crashed into the chain across the east gate. Mister Sam walked slowly, nursing a feeling that he had been badly treated: *he* hadn't been told to expect it so if it had driven clear into the chain it wouldn't have been *his* fault, no one had told *him* anything. He still felt he knew too little, only that Mr. Simmons had driven in like a bat out of hell, and then the ambulance like another, to the Faculty House. He'd be damned if he'd ask who it was all for and what it was all about. *Let them come and tell me.*

Beyond the wall to the east, dimly, he could still see Millicent. She seemed to be moving slowly, gracefully, like some fey creature in a dream ballet, around the gray telephone pole. He could not see her face, only her willowy, indistinct outline as it dipped and straightened, moving in a fantastic circle. *Dotty*, he thought, and moved along on his tour.

The doors at Elias Cook were still unlocked. He knocked and waited for the matron to come. Awful fog tonight, he planned to remark to her, but she looked grim and tired when she opened the door.

"Everybody to home?"

"Yes. Thank you, Mister Sam. I'm just locking up."

"Hear about the commotion up to Faculty House?"

"Yes. I did. Well, goodnight, Mister Sam."

Tight-mouthed old hen. Hell with her. Don't give a damn what goes on in this hole full of females. Let 'em all get toted off for all I care. Testing the chain across the west gate, Mister Sam sent his light into dim corners to the right and left, and continued his disgruntled inspection tour of the wall.

Just beyond the reach of his flashlight, Trudy Langer, Nan Kittredge and Ruthie Vandermeer sat on the backsteps of Elias Cook whispering, their arms clasping their knees. They could not have explained it, but as soon as the matron had locked the doors they felt compelled to leave their legal, safe perch on the second-floor fire escape and climb down to the steps, which were out of bounds at this hour. For them, rebellion took this accepted form: they were physically outside the prescribed area.

"Johanna's theory is that someone *died*," whispered Nan.

"Tough rocks. I'll cry tomorrow. . . . In *this* place? Not damn likely. That's the trouble with it, no one ever does. They all

live on a coupla centuries and then are immediately reincar-
nated into headmistresses or matrons or something." The scab
on Trudy's leg had healed lightly. Now she began to loosen it,
enjoying the darkness which left her free to pursue her pleasure.

"Who's going to the mixer tomorrow evening?" asked Nan,
who could not think too long about the possibilities of near
death.

"I've got that stupid oaf, George Ryan, and I'd just as leave
not go," said Ruthie.

The blood came. Trudy said, feeling it warm on her finger:
"I'm going with Jamie Roebling."

The astonishment of her friends was gratifying. In the dark
they seemed to be trying to see her, glorified for the first time.
Tomorrow they'd find out the truth, but tonight, in this brief
moment in the darkness, with the enlarged raw sore of her
leg beginning already to clot—by tomorrow when she again
needed its solace she could pick it again—she sat bathed in
congratulations and self-admiration.

"God, I'm glad that acceptance came. I had visions of never
getting out of here. A lifetime member. I can't wait to see the
last of this place."

"What do you think it'll be like?" asked Ruthie.

"What?"

"College."

"Oh about the same as every other place. Work. Rules. A
coupla people you like and who don't know you're alive, and a
thousand you despise. Rankins and Sewards all over the place."

"Sewards? Why Sewards?"

"Oh, I don't know. She's the kind of loony crumb that I
bet you find everywhere in schools. It's prolly like Cadmus and
those dragon teeth he sowed that came up soldiers. These educational types spring up everywhere. I bet you. Well, I've had it.
Let's go up. God, what a day."

"How do you mean?" asked Ruthie, hungry for a little more
gossip.

"Hot, and all that."

"Above all we must not alarm the students."

In their shock united for once, the teachers seated around the mahogany table in the sitting room nodded to the Headmistress. Tonight they clung to the table like shipwrecked survivors of a storm. Ever since Jo had poured hot water into the cups containing powdered coffee or dangling tea bags no one had uttered a word. Only Mrs. Bache was absent from the hastily gathered faculty, for in the presence of still another death her legs had given way under her, and she had to be helped to her room. When Robbie and Meg left her she was speaking low in German to herself, her exhausted shoulders slanted toward the ground. Still in German she had asked Meg to bring her her books which she'd left downstairs. Meg said she would and not to worry about them. Before the door closed, relieved of her major worry, Mrs. Bache had fallen asleep, still sitting up on her bed.

"Above all else, we must avoid publicity. At least until after school closes. Do you think that's possible, Miss Rankin?"

Miss Rankin had handled all publicity emanating from the school ever since the time a former science teacher had allowed a photographer to publish some rather indecorous pictures taken in the girls' dormitory.

"We can try. I'll get in touch with Ernie Keating who handles our releases and ask him what he can do for us."

The telephone rang. Miss Rankin, almost too quickly, went into the hall to answer it. After a moment she returned and gestured to Miss Blount who went out after her, her tall, spare body at its usual hurried slant, her hair in turmoil.

Jo said, more to break the introspective silence than to be of service: "More coffee, anyone?"

No one answered. Each teacher was sunk, isolated, into a private, cold, bare examination room of her own, in which she sat, out of contact and grotesquely alone, trying to make some order and reason out of the day's progress into the tragedy of this evening. Robbie and Jo sat together, in the greatest isolation of all, for they longed to restore their broken contact with each other but were forced to remain alone, in tortuous chambers of memory, exploring. To Robbie the white look of rejection on Jo's face was terrifying. She forced herself to retrace her steps, to journey up and down the corridors of this fearful day: the moment in bed this morning when she first became aware of Jo's plan to invite Sophie, *I've something to say to you, did she say, just before, or just after, she closed the window?* Robbie dug down fiercely into her memory, looking for the moment, the *exact* time when her resolve to block the visit had been formed. In bed, hot, the thought of the whole day ahead too much for her, *was that the moment of guilt? the carillon ringing and Jo newly washed at the window, walking from the window, arise my love. Did I say to myself at that moment: I will not let her come, I will not suffer the fool gladly, did I then determine the gross black tongue and the bleeding throat that I saw tonight, perhaps shall always see?* To Robbie it seemed imperative that she pinpoint the instant she had entered decisively into the dead woman's destiny because vaguely she felt that somewhere she must share in the blame. *I started it all perhaps, is that why I must know?* Her jaw set against the thought, depressed, looking sullen, she fought hard against the realization that the web of motives she had for so long ignored included her own, inescapably. Lowering the scalpel gently into the next layer she asked herself about the cost of the tragedy: *was I only, oh God let it be so, a supporting player, or the main part? I didn't want her around, it comes to that. I wanted Jo to myself. I thought, after all my long time alone, in my unknown and special kind of loneliness, I was entitled to her special company. All the rest of the year I pay dearly for my peculiar preference. I bend and give, I cover and hide, I pretend and even lie, because the truth is fatal to me and openness will strip me bare. She threatened us, our relationship. Certainly. That was it. Everyone and everything threatens it because it exists on a rare plane and to invoke Jo's sympathy and concern was to deplete my share, and what would have been left for me who can feed nowhere else, not in any of the standard, regular tables.*

Sophie's presence, in our free time, seemed to me—and was—a public notice that our magic circle was imperfect. So I acted in the only way I know how, to plug the threatened gap, to complete the imperfect arc. I gave Jo what I knew to be (for us, for her) an impossible choice. I cut the threat of infection out, expelled the undesirable element, the flaw in the pattern.

What have I really done? Prevented a small unkindness in the light of greater future damage. I cannot be blamed, when you come to think of it clearly, for what happened, and I will not blame myself. My guilt (if I have any) is an older one in the modern social sense, but the fourth-century before the Christian era Greek would not have condemned me. In any other sense I am not to be blamed, nor is my ally. I held what was perilously mine against the threat of an invader. The method may have been harsh but like all occupations one may be permitted some emergency measures. . . .

She smiled at Jo who sat rigid beside her. Jo would not return the smile. A little pile of quizzes reflected itself in the surface of the mahogany table in front of Jo. She rested her head on her finger tips, trying to concentrate on the top paper. But the blurred reflection of her own pale and ghostly face in the marred surface of the table would not let her work. The pained reflection puzzled her: why am I so down? A sense of complicity in tonight's terrible tableau lay like a shawl about her neck, pressing down on her shoulders and reducing, curiously, the flow of blood to her face. Confused by doubts during the last two hours, in Jo's mind the death of Sophie had become a personal failure. She had retreated in time back into her hospitable familial past. She saw her family and its visitors and permanent guests, her friends and the friends of her friends, seated around the expandable dining-room table. Her father hoots with pleasure at a remark made by a visiting boy halfway down the table, and the laugh is caught and echoed and bandied down one side, crosses at the lower end, leaping then over the barricade of bread and gravy and sliced meat, like a forest fire crossing a break. Her mother tries to quiet the little ones, fearing for their digestion she says reproachfully to her husband, but her calm voice disappears into the general uproar that flickers, almost goes out and then flares again at the top of the table. Absent-mindedly they all eat mountains of food, although it is hard to catch anyone in the act of bringing it up to his mouth: so high and wild and constant is the talk and the laughter. Intense affection flows out freely even toward the friends of friends and the guests one never saw before this day, and Jo feels the old pride in her gay father, her brothers and sisters, her quietly amused mother. Now she understood her sin tonight: a failure in hospitality, a narrowing of the hearth to its owners, a closing of shutters, a withdrawal of the bridge across the moat. Desperately shaken by her thoughts she went on exploring the dining room of her memory, the glow of pleasure from its gaiety that she still retained.

But then again, she couldn't have known. She must have died thinking she was still coming to the Cape. Was there a hint anywhere from her that it might involve some trouble with Robbie? I don't think so. Could she have heard us? . . . No that's impossible. She never knew. And if I failed it was an unknown failure, known only to me and Robbie who cannot blame me for anything. It was for her I did it, for her troubled look and her continuous loneliness. And if it wasn't known then it couldn't have been the cause or even part of the cause and so I am not guilty. Exonerated now in every sense.

Jo looked up and saw Robbie smiling at her. Pushing the pile of untouched quizzes away from her, she smiled back. Cleared of levees of debris, the rubble of doubt raked into the dim corners of the sitting room where no lights burned, the two resumed their tacit unity, complacent, resolved, one.

Miss Blount and Miss Rankin, looking disturbed, filed back. The coroner's report had been released to the *Newton News* man who called to get details. Miss Blount had asked Miss Rankin to handle him. Miss Rankin, cold and correct, had said there was little she could add to the coroner's report, no, there had been no note. She had added, to be rid of the persistent

Mr. Tweed was it? that Miss Seward had been quite well and no one at the school knew of any reason why Miss Seward should have wished to take her life. . . .

"Unfortunately," finished Miss Rankin, "Mr. Keating has gone on his vacation."

"Now the second thing we must discuss is what we shall tell the students," said Miss Blount. Her voice was hoarse with weariness. "Something must be explained to them."

Meg Miers nodded and then wondered why she had. She spread her fingers apart along the dark edge of the table. They were too numb to hold a sketching pencil, too strained to hold anything ever again, she thought. *When would the feel of the rope wear away, the lush overflowing feel of flesh just recently dead wear away: why do tactile sensations cloy so and visual ones disappear so quickly? If I wanted to I could not sketch her now as she was as late as this afternoon, because my mind is totally occupied by the horror of her newly dead face abandoned to that deep flush of violent suffocation. I should have asked her earlier to come to the Studio to talk when Ellen came, I should have offered her an escape hatch. Why didn't I? Because I was absorbed in the surfaces I am always trying to catch. Because Ellen was composed and did not enlist my aid I chose her for my private consolation and comfort. The Studio is a place of privacy, Sophie apparently needed some, an escape into company, and I never thought of it. Is that a fault? Am I guilty of her end tonight?*

There is this, however. The practice of an art demands removal, distance. One cannot take a chance on being upset so that the fingers freeze and the mind decomposes into inaccurate edges and indistinct shades. Art is too miserly to afford sympathy if events diminish the artist and too egotistical to allow him to be always sensitive to another's needs. The choice, had I thought to make it, was actually between me and her. I cannot be blamed for choosing myself. At the moment when Meg took Sophie's dead-weight body down from the rafter her feeling of complicity underneath was strongest. But slowly, judged in the light of her later thought, it had grown less and less until now, upon the realization of the absolute demands of the one thing that mattered to Meg, she had satisfied herself, and was once more at peace. If she had had a pencil with her at this moment of reconciliation with herself she would have removed her frozen fingers from the table, where she sat transfixed like a Ouija-board player, and begun a small sketch, Goya-esque as she now suddenly saw it, of the group around the table.

The telephone rang, stirring the inert teachers to mutters of irritation. Upstairs the distant, persistent ringing woke Mrs. Bache abruptly from a profound sleep. *That poor woman. If I had but known she was suffering. I might have told her my autobiography to console her, to let her know she was not alone. The skeleton-woman I slept beside in one camp who pinched herself hard all night to feel anything, something, pain, the sense of life. The evening my husband was pulled away from the wire fence and left his thumb on it, and the last I saw of him, bleeding lieber Gott, nothing but great eyes and tears and blood. So many like her in despair in that place and other places, who died although they tried so hard to live and others who died because their wish to live had been smothered in filth and starvation and disgust: hearing of this, might it not have helped her to feel the comradeship of the despondent, the friendship that the traditionally disinherited feel for each other? Had she been a Jew she might have been accustomed to the ancient sense of separation from the majority, she might have been toughened to hurt. That poor woman. Alone. And not used to it.* This unaccustomed excursion into another human being, after so long, tired the science teacher. She kicked off her shoes and settled back into the same position. Almost immediately she was sunk into her usual troubled sleep into which she had managed to relegate her unspeakable memories.

"Could we say she had been . . . suddenly called away?" Madame Mifflin suggested to the Headmistress. Her bright eyes looked oddly blunted and dull, and for the first time in her bustling day the ring in her voice promised no significant disclosures.

"I think not. They must have seen the cars and the ambulance. They know something more than that has happened," said Miss Rankin. She managed to make the timbre of her voice suggest her scorn of Madame's suggestion.

"I suggest we announce at the beginning of Station Church tomorrow that Miss Seward died suddenly of heart failure, and that we offer some prayers for her. When we find out where her brother wishes to have the burial we can let the students send flowers to the funeral."

"I think that's wise, Miss Rankin," said the Headmistress, heartened by this view she had just been given of a way out of her predicament. "I feel that the more casual we are about it the better. But even flowers might prolong the talk too long and might . . . set a precedent we wouldn't want to keep up. Let's just limit our sorrow to the prayers at Church in the morning. I hope Our Maestro is on time for once. And I'll speak to Reverend Wilbur when he comes for breakfast."

"He's a fine man. He'll handle it well." Madame Mifflin's reverence for the Newton minister was well-known. Primarily she admired him for not being a priest, and for being what she called "a free man of God." Having spoken once and righteously, she retired into a gloom she rarely encountered in her usual thoughts. In this unwonted depression she looked at herself as a Bushman does into a mirror, for the first time. Newly, unaccustomedly introspective, there formed before her eyes the quick, black, darting easy pleasures of her hitherto wholly verbal life, bilingual, sharp: the sly, the nasty, the insinuating, the suggestive—all the thousands of words she had used to wing, to reduce, to bring down, to maim. Since the death this evening she had been tortured by a new vision: she saw them returned to her, concretized into instruments of torture, inflicted upon the suffused face of Sophie Seward. She questioned herself, like a cross-examiner seeking a perjury victim, about what she had said to Sophie in the last days: *was I somehow implicated in Sophie's decision?* She found the thought terrifying. She had not the strength, the inner resources for so great a burden. Everywhere in her shocked and shallow mind, inundated with words she had spoken with intent or without it, she sought escape: words spoken, words forgotten, words meant to be spoken. In every direction she sought escape from responsibility.

Oh Sophie, if it was the talk of my children, the stories about them while you were childless, listen to me. Pauvre amie. Veuillez m'ecouter: Je n'ai pas d'enfants! *I have no one. No Dorothea. No Jean. I made them up. Created them. So I would not be . . . so vulnerable to parents, to the families all around me everywhere. On the faculty. At Church. Children everywhere. Oh Sophie, I have sinned against you by my stories, my talk,* mes verbes. Mea culpa. Mea maxima culpa.

To the stunned surprise of the teachers at the table, Maddame's traditional Gallic *savoir-faire*, her solid self-assurance, cracked suddenly: aloud she said, "Miséricorde," put her head down on the polished table and wept, high, gasping sobs. No one moved to comfort her. Under the measureless seas of their own isolations, each one within herself wept with her. Madame's strange breakdown was merely the outward show of an inner, general lamentation.

"One other thing," continued the Headmistress inexorably, ignoring the weeping French mistress. "The parents. If they inquire, when they come for Weekend, we must explain that their daughters' reports are exaggerated—emotional effusions of the very young. It would be very serious if the idea got about that the faculty was composed of mentally unstable members."

Lucy Moore, who rarely spoke at any faculty gathering, could bear the funereal atmosphere no longer. She had hardly known Sophie; and her youth and health protected her from the general sense of tragedy that the others now shared. Vaguely she regretted that anyone who possessed life should find it preferable to be without it (the sun, the lovely spring air, the sense of rightness in one's muscles, running, hitting, the white ball, the feel of ice water afterwards down one's face, the backswing, the easy, loping forehand), but she felt more comfortable in the present and even safer in thoughts of the future.

"With no classes this week," she said quietly, "would you think it might be a good idea to distract the lower classmen, while the seniors are rehearsing for Commencement, by organizing some sports and things? We could have a tennis tourney, some field hockey—even a field day towards the end of the week, if you thought it a good idea."

"Very good. Very good," said the Headmistress, absently. "Anything at all."

Miss Rankin opened her large, yellow folder and ticked off items. "As long as nothing interferes with our use of the fields when we need to rehearse the Procession outside, and the gym and auditorium for the indoor parts. According to the schedule a good time would be . . ."

They were off. Like mourners who have sat too long at a bier they had slipped back from the solemn levels of the occasion into everyday matters, being too small, too human to stay aloft so long. They talked of tomorrow and Station Church, they planned the afternoon following it and the evening, in unaccustomed detail for a Sunday. Miss Rankin, back in her element, made notations on the papers in her folder. Lucy yawned in pleasant weariness from today's tennis, her inner self laved by the thought of so many athletic events in the week ahead, *so much sun—a lovely burn to start my sailing days next week.* The plans expanded into marching orders; they spoke indirectly, tentatively, Miss Rankin emphasized, of packing, closing the Art Studio and Library for the summer ("I will put up an order of return for books, so that each class will arrive at a given time," Miss Rankin said to Ellen, who handled these details in the Library and who had made no contribution to the discussions). It was now ten o'clock, a cool breeze moved the elderly curtains into the room, a light on the far side wall caught Miss Hands's admonishing finger and held it fixed, aimed directly at the group huddled about the table. (Meg thought: we are by Van Gogh—*The Miners at a Table*, was it?)

"Before we adjourn for the night I should like to say one thing." Miss Blount stood up, assuming moral command by her elevated position over the group and by her standard compassionate expression. Her neck bore its heavy veins at a tired angle, making her great height seem stringy, almost loose. A disarranged Brobdingnagian, she held her empty cup and rose above them, the tone of her voice suggesting a promise of escape, of amnesty, from their private captivities:

"We have nothing whatever to blame ourselves for. We all did our best for her, all along the line. Our first duty was and always is to the girls, and she was in every way a threat to the performance of that duty. *She* provoked *them*. So I want each of you to get a good night's sleep, forget what has happened tonight and prepare yourselves to meet the girls in Church tomorrow with cheerful, calm faces."

Ellen said, aloud to herself, fixedly looking at no one: "We all have sufficient strength to support the misfortunes of others."

"What was that?" rapped Miss Rankin.

"De la Rochefoucauld," replied Ellen in the same suffocated tone.

Everyone but Ellen stood up and began to file out, their faces, even Madame's white, drawn one, studiously wiped of all emotion, as if they all were, in obedience to the Headmistress, practicing their expressions for tomorrow. The Headmistress flicked the lights twice. Robbie shut her lips hard, visibly repressing her customary comment. Miss Blount said:

"Coming, Miss Acton?"

Ellen, still seated, nodded. "In a few moments, Miss Blount. You can douse the lights. It's cooler."

"Goodnight. Please be sure the stairs light and the porch light are out when you come up."

"Yes." Ellen waved her head slightly. No more words would come. She felt she could not force them forth; of only that single monosyllable was she now capable.

As they walked together toward the stairs, Miss Rankin, her voice pitched so low that it was almost inaudible to the Headmistress, said:

"Quite frankly, I feel no guilt whatsoever in this matter. Only a coward or a weakling," she hesitated for a moment, another vision suddenly, frighteningly, superimposing itself unbidden upon that of Sophie and the trench-coat belt red with Meg Meirs's blood: the shower rail wrenched away from the wall . . . "would take her own life." She was aware that her voice, strangely out of control, had risen sharply and that she was now almost shouting, but she felt powerless to quiet it. "How can we be held responsible for the inherent weaknesses of others?" she demanded loudly of the startled Headmistress. Miss Blount did not reply. Speaking to the teachers she had been sure of her thoughts, but in Miss Rankin's mouth her words took on a dismayingly sour edge.

They climbed together. Miss Rankin pulled her heavy earrings from the lobes of her ears. Her tiredness was to be witnessed only in that small area of her body. Beside her white face the lobes looked as if all her blood had been concentrated in them.

Miss Rankin glanced back at Ellen left alone in the dying light and ancient splendor of the sitting room. Ashamed of her lapse, she leaned closer to the Headmistress and said hoarsely but low: "Miss Acton worries me, Miss Blount. She seems . . . rather disturbed these days. Her cynicism is, well, unhealthy and . . . dangerous for a faculty like ours. I think she must be watched closely, and next year, if she persists . . ." The Assistant was afraid to go further into the sensitive no-mans-land of contracts and hiring.

"I know. It *is* too bad. These days—Commencement and all —is usually our happy time. But you're right, I'm sure. We can no longer be sure of her . . . her *loyalty*. It may well be time to . . ."

They stood together on the landing before their rooms, the subject of Ellen's disenchantment with the Handian myth hovering delicately, unspoken, between them. Then, and with a certain smugness, the Headmistress said:

"Did you receive an invitation to Priscilla Ames's wedding on the 26th, I think, of next month?"

"*Eleanor* Ames."

"Yes, Eleanor."

"The twenty-sixth. That's a Friday. Strange day for it," said Miss Rankin, who had calculated rapidly, dazzlingly, to be able to deflect the negative answer with her mental gymnastics.

Routed but still pleased, the Headmistress retreated with dignity. "Oh, that may be the wrong date. Sometime around there, however."

"I did not. She never liked me, as I remember. Nor I her."

"Is that right?" said the Headmistress, mechanically. She nodded goodnight and went into her room. A terrible, terrible day. But over now. Kicking off her shoes she wearily watched one fall under the bed. She stretched her feet luxuriously and then started to prepare for the night. As she shed the confines of her clothes, her body and her old, tired mind together slowly sank into a blissful, thoughtless ease.

Feeling exposed even in the dark, Ellen stood up and walked to her morning seat behind the door. She switched on the table lamp at her right, her elbow disturbing the balance of Mrs. Bache's books stacked beside her; she caught them just in time. Idly, to distract herself from the tumultuous upstairs sounds of water rushing, doors closing abruptly and padded feet moving back and forth to the bathroom, she opened the top one, a heavy, formidable book called *Modern Physical Theory*. Page after page of charts, graphs and formulae, of words of unknown meaning to Ellen in their specific sense or even, she thought grimly, in their vague and general sense. *I am one of C. P. Snow's scientific illiterates, but it's too late now to re-educate me.*

She opened, instinctively, to the back end-papers of the book she held, where she remembered Mrs. Bache translated her private sorrows into quotations. A three-by-five card dropped out, and Ellen read aloud from it, stopping often to decipher the tight German script:

> Oh Rose thou art sick!
> The invisible worm
> That flies in the night
> In the howling storm,
>
> Has found out thy bed
> Of crimson joy,
> And his dark secret love
> Does thy life destroy.

Ellen shut *Modern Physical Theory*, slamming it. The sound echoed in the far corners of the empty sitting room. Across the campus the carillon sounded but whether for eleven or twelve she was now too weary, too far from reality, to tell. The strain of this St. Gregory's feast day, the invisible worm in the heart of the lost Junior English Mistress, the day's violent reminder of her own insufficiency, gathered about the embattled Ellen who sat motionless, weighing her chances of escape from guilt. At five-thirty or so she had become part of a murder, a member of the suicide, at the moment that she turned away, knowing she was needed. Now she knew, and it was too late for motion. Then she had known and had done nothing. Sophie had needed moral adrenalin, a hand, a hope, a word, any word at five o'clock this afternoon and I, steeped in my careful, selective, protective Christianity, full to the teeth with dogmatic theory and catechism and mental prayers and penances and liturgy and the hope of indulgences, I went to dinner, to the Buttery, to the trough, to feed my self-possession and lounge untroubled at dessert and coffee.

Is there an excuse? Can I free myself? Love thee one another. No. I am Horatio, witness for Sophie, but she never waited to ask: "and in this harsh world draw thy breath in pain to tell my story." Let us greet the students tomorrow with whimpers and worms and buskin, with crosses low and obscure on the bosom. God. God. I cannot escape, ever. I must do penance until this cul-de-sac of self opens into nothingness or something, now at the hour of my death, I lent her ten dollars and worried today, at the hour of her death, about getting it back. *Quand même.* I never *did* count the *Macbeths* in the book closet. Did I get all the copies back? . . . . And the Headmistress reminds us that when they are most unlovable . . . and I remind her that we shall none of us ever be entirely free again. We are inextricably bound for the first time each to the other by the steel wires of a trench-coat belt. "Take up the bodies. . . ."

For Swift writes to Stella, I remember, something like: "I hate life when I think it exposed her (Lady Something or other) to such accident; and to see so many thousand wretches burdening the earth, while such as her die, makes me think God did never intend life for a blessing." I shall go up now that it's quieted down and fall hard on my knees and say the first genuine act of contrition I have ever made to God . . . the invisible worm that flies in the night to God from me and my inescapable, unchristian, everlasting moment of guilt . . . and finish my Comments and brush my teeth and put something down in my notebook. . . .

Ellen became aware of footsteps on the stairs. Meg appeared out of the darkness of the hall.

"I forgot. I promised Mrs. Bache to bring up her books."

"They're here."

"Coming?"

"With you." Ellen snapped out the lamp and walked with Meg to the stairs. They climbed slowly. At the landing Ellen turned to Meg, patted her shoulder and smiled, inexplicably, said goodnight, and opened the door to her room.